T0149641

KATRINA'S
JUSTICE

KATRINA'S JUSTICE

K.R. FISCHER

KATRINA'S JUSTICE

iUniverse books may be ordered through booksellers or by contacting:

iUniverse
1663 Liberty Drive
Bloomington, IN 47403
www.iuniverse.com
1-800-Authors (1-800-288-4677)

ISBN: 978-1-5320-7877-4 (sc)
ISBN: 978-1-5320-7878-1 (e)

Library of Congress Control Number: 2019910177

Print information available on the last page.

iUniverse rev. date: 07/19/2019

Hope

"Of all the forces that make for a better world, none
is so powerful than hope. With hope,
One can think, one can work, and one can dream.
If you have hope, you have everything."

Author-unknown

I would like to thank personally my mother, Dana Fischer who took the time to edit and inspire me to write this book. I would also like to thank my children Michael, Joseph and Elizabeth in all the support they showed while working on this book.

I would like to thank Ipublishing and its supportive staff especially Krista who helped motivate me to complete the book.

THE PSYCHIATRIST OFFICE was on the second floor of an older style home in the downtown area. There was a small reception area with a few chairs and in the corner a small child's table with two chairs. On top of the child's table a container filled with all sizes and colors of crayons along a selection of coloring books and storybooks. By one of the adult chairs a small corner table had a selection of magazines and information booklets for parents' to read. Katrina Garret was carrying her daughter Rosa in her arms, while Wayne and Junior quickly ran up the stairs to the top. Dean was following all of them and he was carrying a large baby bag. They had just made it in time for their evening appointment and Katrina was signing on the clip board. She had just sat down and put little Rosa back on her lap to read a story and the boys had begun coloring in one of the coloring books. A shorter than average man who was fairly thin, bald and wore wired glasses came into the room to introduce himself as the psychiatrist that was going to be testing Junior for attention deficit and attention hypertension deficit disorders.

"Hello everyone my name is Doctor Emit McDoodle; I will be the one that will be conducting the necessary testing on Junior, but first I need to talk to you Mrs. Garret since you probably have the family's medical history. This way I can get an idea about their family life."

She nodded her head in a yes manner while putting Rosa down in the chair next to Dean and then got up to introduce her family and shakes the hand of Dr. McDoodle. "Hello Dr. McDoodle, please call me Katrina this is Wayne, Junior the one you are seeing and Rosa; my husband Dean. Since, I have Junior's pediatrician records along with other family's medical history and behavior information."

Dr. McDoodle agreed with Katrina, "Will you please follow me to my office so we can discuss the concerns that you have and the preschool report has about Junior's actions."

Katrina responded in a quick manner, to Dean "Will you be alright with the children while I take a few minutes to talk with Dr. McDoodle and give him the papers the preschool had given her for the appointment."

Dean looked up at her, "yes we will be fine." Then he returned to reading the story to Rosa and Wayne had climbed in the other chair beside him listening to the story. Katrina handed the folder to Dr. McDoodle when they entered the room. Katrina looked over the room. Dr. McDoodle had sat down in a large roller desk chair by an old dark wood desk that took up the entire wall. The office was decorated in a southwest motif. There were two big comfy chairs for parents' to sit in and on the other side shelves that went from the floor to the ceiling. The lower shelves had Lego sets for children to play along with reading books for all ages, board games, beads, counting flash cards, and puzzles. The higher shelves had medical books, parent information pamphlets, the latest medicine books and many other books.

Katrina had taken a seat and waited patiently for Dr. McDoodle to look over the information she had just handed him. He was taking notes in a stenographer notebook and was flipping through each page.

When Dr. McDoodle finally looked up from the papers, "Katrina, why don't you go and bring Junior back here so I can see how he interacts with some of my testing. He will think that he is playing with puzzles."

Katrina left the office room and found Junior still at the small children's' table building a Lego contraption. "Junior why don't you come with me and you can bring that with you; Dr. McDoodle would like to see you." She took Junior's hand and walked back to the room.

Once inside the room, Junior began to talk about what he made with the toy to him. "This is a truck and it can fly see the wings," Junior talked in a fast pace and Dr. McDoodle listened.

"Junior why don't you put it here and here is something else for you to build. Katrina you may leave us now while I get to know him better and I will let him come to you in about a half-an-hour." Katrina got up from her seat and shut the door behind her, then walked down to where Dean, Wayne and Rosa were in the waiting room.

"Mommy, I'm getting hungry can we go to get something to eat?" Wayne was whining.

"Dean, I may have some snacks in the van look under the second seat for a small cooler; there might be a few juice boxes along with snackables for the kids." She said with ease. Dean put Rosa down and held her tiny hand. Wayne began climbing down the stairs, too. They were gone for awhile and before long Junior came out running from the room toward Katrina.

"Whoa, buddy slow down," He came to a quick halt, "mommy the doctor needs you," and grabs her hand.

Katrina and Junior went back together to Dr. McDoodle's room. Dr. McDoodle was waiting for her and Junior. "I would like to schedule another appointment for Junior to finish the last part of the testing.

It should take at least an hour to complete and then I can give your family my recommendations." She looked at the calendar, "I think next Saturday late morning will work for everyone, since my husband will be driving us here." She answered Dr. McDoodle.

"This way Dean wouldn't have to take a half-day from his work," Katrina replied.

Dr. McDoodle looked over the other scheduled appointments of his patients. "Yes, that will work; I have no other appointments scheduled until after two that afternoon." While both adults penciled in the appointment time for the upcoming Saturday morning at eleven.

Junior said a quick, "good-bye" to Dr. McDoodle and ran out into the waiting room; and she commented a quick thank you then began to walk briskly to the waiting room to catch up with Junior before he went downstairs to catch up with Dean, Wayne, and Rosa. She would suggest that they should stop at a family restaurant to feed everyone before heading home that night. Deep down Katrina was hoping that Junior and Rosa would fall asleep in their car seats on the return trip home. They ate dinner and began the trip home. They would take the same rural state road home that Dean had taken on the way to the appointment which would be over an hour drive. Dean was paying attention to the road. She took a look behind her to check on the children since they were so quiet. All of them had fallen asleep to the sound of the moving van. Although, the last weather report that she heard from the van radio just hours ago was calling for 6 to 8 inches of new snow west of the city. She was hoping that the weather would hold out until they arrived home. Katrina looked out the van window and all she could see for miles was abandon corn or soy fields with farm houses. Some of the farm houses that she saw had a small dim light inside to show someone was still awake but other than that all that could be seen was a clear winter sky with several twinkling stars. She knew that with no clouds that the temperature would drop below freezing overnight.

"By the way Dean I scheduled the next appointment for this Saturday in the late morning for Dr. McDoodle to finish the testing on Junior. This way you won't have to take any time off from work," she stated.

"That's fine, I guess," was all that Dean said. Katrina reached over to the van radio and turned on some music with a very low volume so that the children would not be woken up. Dean turned his head just enough toward Katrina with his eyes still on the road.

"You knew from the very beginning how I did not want to spend so much time commuting to work, especially away from civilization. People at work say I live in the boondocks and they have never even heard of the town that we live in," his voice sounded more than irritated.

Katrina knew that he wasn't happy about moving further west, but the houses that they had seen in the past few weeks either was out of their price ranger or just did not have enough rooms. The other important factor was that Katrina did not want to make too many changes all at once because she wanted the children to keep somewhat the same daily schedule. That would mean to keep the same pediatrician that they had since the day they were born.

They had decided to put up the starter home for sale shortly after the Christmas holidays. She thought by placing the small house up on the real estate market during the holiday's that it would not sale quickly. Unfortunately, the house sold quicker than everyone could dream of and now the search for the right house for their family. They would need to search for a home with one criteria being; it would also need to be empty. Dean after work had met her at several houses to look at with Mr. Alex Basil, their real estate agent. Many of the houses that they had looked at was not in their budget and some even had people still living in them.

4

Dean checked his cell phone messages and Mr. Basil had called while the family was at the appointment and left a message on the answering machine. Katrina liked Mr. Alex Basil.

His message stated, "I might have found another home for both of you to look at but it is a little further west than what you wanted. It is in a nice area with some new construction and the area use to be a vacation place that started to build residential housing. The house is empty and the construction company is looking for a buyer. Call me back if you are interested and we can schedule a time to view it."

Katrina knew from the very beginning that if the family moved further west that Dean would commute at least an hour if not more because of road construction. Although it was further in distance the amount of time was still the same. It was that the size of the house was just right for the family budget. Dean had a problem dealing with abnormalities no matter who they were including his son Junior.

"Really would it kill you if you actually showed your son that you cared?" Katrina took a deep breath and sighed. Dean didn't respond right away, as he was focused on the two lane country road.

He glanced over to Katrina just for a few seconds and then went back to looking at the road. The roads were a little slippery from the dusting of the snow. Katrina went back to looking out of the caravan window and drifted off to sleep. When she awoke Dean was pulling the caravan into the organized garage. She opened the caravan door and grabbed the large diaper bag along with her purse. Then she proceeded to open the door of the house into a foyer and turning on some of the lights. Dean followed her into the house carrying Wayne in his arms and went directly to Wayne's bedroom. She sat the diaper bag and purse onto the oak entry table before returning to the caravan to get Rosa out of her car seat. Dean quickly undressed Wayne and put a pair of Thomas pajamas on then tucked him into bed. Katrina carried Rosa into her pink bedroom then changed her into a princess nightgown for bed. Rosa was rubbing her eyes with her hands. Katrina knew that she would be wide awake if she didn't rock Rosa back to sleep. She was glad that they had put the old fashion wooden rocker in Rosa's bedroom. Katrina rocked Rosa to sleep and began to hum a lullaby. Dean had taken Junior out of the caravan and changed him into a pair of pajamas and tucked him into bed. She could here in the distance the television had been turned on in the master bedroom. She had gotten Rosa back to sleep and carried her to the toddler bed and tucked her in hopefully for the night. Tonight after the doctor visit Katrina knew they were both too exhausted and went to bed. Dean would need to get up early to get the snow blower out to plow the driveway before leaving for the long drive into the suburbs for work.

The new house actually looked much smaller on the outside compared to the inside. There were a lot of rooms along with a wooded area in the backyard for the children to play. Katrina had been busy after the Christmas holidays painting some of the rooms. She had painted Rosa's bedroom first by painting one wall a light pink. Then she had taken another wall and painted little pink and white bows across the entire wall. She had finished painting just over a week ago with the bedroom and Dean went to a local department store to pick up a pink toddler bed. Katrina was going to start in the hall way bathroom decorating with Dalmatian pups from the Walt Disney movie. Katrina had finished unpacking from the move except for some boxes that were in the basement. As you came into the house from the front door a staircase went to the second floor where there were three semi-large bedrooms and a bathroom in the hallway. Wayne and Junior had their own bedrooms upstairs and the third bedroom was being used as a playroom. The main floor had a living room with a fire place on the south wall and a large picture window facing the street. The dining room was just to the left of the living room and a kitchen bar separated the formal eating area to the kitchen. In the kitchen, sliding glass doors went out to a large deck facing the wooded area. The english walk out basement was a large room where the family room was with a large entertainment system and theater style television. The laundry room was off to the right along with another full size bathroom. Just off to the left was another room that was designed to be an office or in-laws room. The basement had French style doors into the Florida room where a six person Jacuzzi was for adults only. Katrina was overwhelmed from the move but was settling into the large home and the new community.

Although, Wayne had made some new friends at the elementary school and Junior had started at the local church's preschool program. Katrina still thought that Wayne seemed lonely and thought that she would need to discuss with Dean the possibility of getting a dog or puppy for the children. The only time they truly communicated these days was at night when the children were in bed or if they could get a babysitter to go out for dinner. She finally had the American dream of having a beautiful house and family. There were only a few houses on their block and across the road the big trees had been excavated before the snow began to fall for another new house. In the spring after the last frost the construction crew would be back over there to finish building the house. At the same time she would began the process of landscaping around the house. She would have several flower beds with tulip bulbs, daffodils, irises, hostas, sun flowers, crocuses and lilies planted in them. While waiting for spring she had started some indoor hobbies like scrapbooking and taking classes on photography restoration at a community college on Saturday mornings for the next eight weeks. She was busy looking for a part-time job to give her some extra cash for those yearly vacations the family would be taking to see extended family members. Every day she had been looking in the local paper for a job and a pet. The jobs were there only if you wanted to commute and she had to consider a baby sitter or day care expenses. Something caught her eye in the paper about a local farm having some basset hound puppies for sale. She would wait to call Dean at work around noon to see if she should take the children after school to look at the puppies. She finished feeding Rosa and made herself a sandwich for lunch.

She dialed the number to the office. "Hello babe, I wanted to discuss this with you earlier but we never seem to have time," she explained.

"I think it is time for us to get a family pet, like a puppy where the boys would need to learn how to take care of it and take some responsibility." Katrina took a deep breath as she listened but Dean did not respond right away.

Dean listened to see if Katrina was going to say anything else, he expected that there was more to it.

"Okay, what breed of dog or puppy is it? What is it going to cost me?" He replied.

She responded with some hesitation, Well a near-by farm has them and the price wasn't listed in the paper. However, the other puppies and pets that are listed in the newspaper were priced around the two hundred dollars."

"I don't see why they cost so much but I will leave the decision up to you, but if the puppy is more than two hundred dollars then you will need to wait until tomorrow before getting it, I have to get back to work. I will see you later on tonight. The office has started a new technical project and I will need to work late for the next couple of weeks." he replied.

"Okay, have a nice night honey." She responded and hung up the phone. She took Rosa out of the high chair and put her into the car seat so they could leave to pick up Junior at preschool. After picking up Junior, she took the kids into her bedroom. She set up the VHS player to watch a Disney movie with them on her bed. She was hoping both children would take a nap this afternoon so they could go out to the near-by farm to look at the puppies. They only had about two hours before the bus would drop off Wayne from school. She knew the roads had been plowed so getting there would not be a problem. It would be a nice surprise for the kids, too. Rosa was already asleep and Junior couldn't keep his eyes opened. Finally he was a sleep. She slowly got off the bed and went to clean up the kitchen from lunch. As she was putting the dirty dishes into the dishwasher she looked out the kitchen window. It had started to flurry and the new falling snow covered the wooded area. She glanced at the clock on the microwave and saw that it was almost time for the bus to drop off Wayne. Soon there would be a new member added to the family.

Wayne opened the front door and closed it right away. "Hi mom where is Junior, Wayne said in a loud voice. "SSSSSSSSSH is he still taking his nap; I will get him up in a few minutes.

Here is your afternoon snack" Katrina quietly replied "After you're done eating your snack. I've a surprise for you and junior, "Katrina stated in a calm voice.

"What surprise?" Wayne asked. "You will see, just finish your snack while I go and get Junior and Rosa up from their nap." Katrina replied. Katrina went back into the bedroom but Junior was already awake and I helped him off the bed. Katrina took him into the bathroom.

"Be a big boy and go to the bathroom for mommy," Katrina said in a low voice. She picked up Rosa and carried her into the other bathroom so she could go before they all went on the small adventure.

Junior came running down the hallway. "Mommy Wayne said that you have a surprise for us" Junior said in an enthusiastic voice.

"Yes I do but first we need to get ready because we have to take the car to get there." Katrina answered her son.

Junior went to his room to get his blanket and yelled to Katrina. "Mommy can I take my blankey?" Junior yelled.

"Yes you can take blankey and nothing else. Where we are going is just up the road." Katrina replied. Rosa was rubbing her eyes as she slowly woke up. Katrina needed to put a pull-up on Rosa along with a clean outfit and then her snowsuit. As she was dressing her she gave Rosa a bottle of apple juice.

"Wayne please, help your brother get on his winter boots and jacket. I have Rosa dressed and I'm getting the diaper bag and putting on my winter coat." Katrina said in a motherly voice. Wayne put his snack plate in the kitchen sink and went to help his younger brother get ready.

"Junior where is your other boot?" Wayne asked his younger brother.

"I don't know where it is." Junior replied as he continually looked for the missing boot. He looked under his bed where he puts everything instead of putting things away like he should.

"I found it!" Junior yells out. He quickly slides out from underneath his twin size bed to put the winter boot on. Wayne and Junior come out of the bedroom toward Katrina.

"Mom we are ready to go, "as the boys say it together in unison. Katrina takes the children out into the garage to get in the Caravan and open the garage door. She buckles Rosa into the car seat right behind her while Junior climbs into the booster car seat and buckles with Wayne right next to him.

"Okay is everyone buckled and ready to go?" as she slowly backs out of the garage to head to the farm where the surprise would be waiting for them. Before long she was pulling the Caravan up to a farm with a large red barn. An older gentleman came out of the barn to greet them. Wayne unbuckled Junior from the car seat and she opened the side van door. The boys quickly got of the van while she unbuckle Rosa before lifting her up and sitting her down in the snow. Rosa with her snowsuit on tried to keep her balance before tumbling into the snow. Katrina shut the van door and turned around to walk toward the older gentleman. Katrina shook the gentleman's hand.

"Good afternoon my name is Katrina and these are my children. The taller one is Wayne, this is Junior and this little one is Rosa."

"Good afternoon children my name is farmer Mack and your mother called me early to let me know that you were coming.

"So, why don't you follow me into the barn where they are with their mother out of the wintery weather," Farmer Mack explained. Wayne and Junior ran to the barn with Katrina carrying Rosa and farmer Mack.

"Boys just wait there until the rest of us catch up," she yelled. They were at the barn door and farmer Mack opened the heavy barn door and turned on a light. Katrina put Rosa down and she waddled toward her older brothers that had found six puppies feeding from the mother. Farmer Mack had shut the door behind them and leaned against an old, rickety stable door. While he watched the children.

"Farmer Mack, are the puppies a mix breed or a pure breed?" she asked. The children were sitting on the floor watching the puppies there were several done eating and ready to play. One of the puppies with dark mud colored spots came over to Wayne and Junior. Rosa was petting the top of the head of the puppy and she knelt down.

"Remember that it is a puppy and be gentle while petting it." Another puppy began sniffing around and was interested in what was going on with the puppy next Wayne.

"Mommy, Mommy! look at all the puppies!" Junior exclaimed.

Farmer Mack answered Katrina's earlier question about the breed.

"The puppies are a Bassett and Beagle mix and they are about eight weeks old," he replied. Farmer Mack must have been working out here in the barn before their arrival, because he was wearing a brown pairs of overalls, an orange beanie hat and work boots. The orange beanie was covering his ears but Katrina guessed he was in his late 40's maybe early 50s. The children continued to play with the puppies.

"Okay Wayne and Junior your dad has agreed on letting us get a puppy. However, on one condition is that you boys will need to share on taking care of it. Which means that after school Wayne you will need to walk him and Junior I will show you how to feed him?" She explained. The boys excitedly shook their heads up and down in a yes response. They decided on the first puppy that was covered in the dark muddy spots. Katrina gave Farmer Mack the money for the puppy and thank him. She had a small box for the puppy to lie in at least until they got home. The wind had picked up and the winter sky was again filled with dark clouds. Wayne held the box with two hands and walked to the van. Katrina opened the van door first she put Rosa into the car seat, second she moved the diaper bag onto the floor by the front, third she put Junior into his booster car seat, and then held the box with the puppy while Wayne climbed in next to Junior. Katrina handed the box and puppy to Wayne to hold until they got home. Katrina began to drive away from the farm and waved to the farmer as they left. She was content with the choice they had made, but knew that a puppy was a lot of work.

"Okay everyone, we need to think of a name for the puppy something everyone can say." As she looked into the rearview mirror, she could see both boys were thinking very hard about what she had said.

"How about the name Harry or maybe Spot, "Wayne said in a proud voice.

"No! I don't like the name mommy. What about Fred?" Junior stated.

"Well I can see that the decision for naming the puppy is going to be hard." "We don't need a name right away so we have some time, but mommy will need to take the puppy to the animal doctor for its shots and I will need to give them his name." When the van pulled into the garage it was already dark outside and it was dinnertime. She would call the vetenarian in the morning after the boys were in school to see what shots the puppy would need and the cost. She had decided to feed the children hot dogs with macaroni and cheese. Wayne had taken the box into his room.

"Mommy can I have an old blanket to put into the box so puppy has something to lay on for the night and I gave him one of my small stuffed animals so he won't get lonely when I go to school tomorrow." Wayne asked. Katrina took Rosa out of the high chair and put her into her playpen to play while she cleaned up the kitchen.

"Junior will you go put on your pajamas and Wayne you need to get things ready for school tomorrow."

Wayne responded, "Okay Mom it's taking care of." Once the kitchen was done she got out Rosa's one piece pajamas so she could have a bath before going to bed. Junior came downstairs with his mismatched pajamas on along with a book to read for bedtime. Katrina enjoyed night time when they were all together by the rocking chair in Rosa's room. There she would read several bedtime stories and usually Rosa and Junior would fall asleep before the third book was read. She went into the bathroom to start the bath water to give Rosa her bath. Then she dressed her for bed.

"Wayne will you go and get ready for beds also pick out only one book to read tonight." She stated. The boys usually picked out Thomas the train books for her to read. They were already in the bedroom when she came in to read. Rosa was on her lap with her favorite blanket, Junior had his favorite blanket next to him on the floor, and Wayne was on the floor next to him. Katrina begins reading the short Thomas story. Then she read a few nursery rhymes from the other books. While she read the stories she rocked in a steady pace soon Rosa and Junior was asleep. She put Rosa down in her bed, then picked up Junior and carried him to bed.

Wayne was yawning and she tucked him to bed.

"Good night puppy," Wayne said in a sleepy voice.

The puppy was lying down but Katrina picked him up and carried him outside to go to the bathroom. She would have the chore of training him not to go inside the house. She was also in the process of potty training Rosa and she was only in diapers at night. She carried the puppy back inside and place him back into the box. While getting ready for bed she heard the garage door open Dean was finally home from work. When Dean walked into the bedroom he looked exceptional tired tonight. Dean was about 5'9 in height with sandy brown hair, bright blue eyes and a well groomed mustache with a full beard. He had gained some weight in the years while sitting behind a desk twelve to fourteen hours a day working on writing computer codes for the company. Katrina was always busy with the children but every now and then Dean would take her out on a date and a babysitter would watch the children. The next day was Friday and she would have the same routine. Dean would leave early before everyone else got up for the day. Wayne and Junior were at the table eating breakfast and Rosa was in her high chair.

"Wayne and Junior I think I have came up with the name for the puppy. Wayne, why don't you go and get the puppy after you eat. Bring him in the kitchen so he can eat and here is a bowl of water." She stated.

Wayne finished his cereal and went to get the box and the puppy. Katrina could here both coming down the stairs. The puppy and Wayne came into the kitchen. Wayne took a handful of puppy food and put it into the bowl his mom gave him. The puppy began eating and wagging his tail.

"What do you boys think of the name Peter from the nursery rhyme I read last night?" Wayne and Junior replied at the same time, "We like the name Mom," Peter Puppy what do you think?" The puppy looked up from his bowl and wagged his tail.

"I think he likes the name too Mommy, Junior said in a happy voice.

"Wayne go brush your teeth, because the bus will be here in a few minutes." His mom stated. She looked out the front window to look for the bus. Wayne grabbed his back pack, zipped up his winter jacket, put on a pair of mittens and hat then went out the door to go to the corner where the bus picked him with three other children that lived nearby. She watched the bus leave the corner bus stop from the door and then took out the puppy to go to the bathroom. Rosa was whining to get out of her high chair.

"Just a minute, I will be there in a minute." The puppy ran back into the house and slid on the ceramic floor. Katrina followed Peter Puppy into the kitchen where he was licking the floor where Rosa had dropped a few of her cheerios. Katrina wiped off Rosa and took her out of the highchair.

"Rosa goes along playing with her toys and with her brother." Junior was already playing with his matchbox cars on the rug that looked like a city. Katrina was already in the process of making her phone calls for the morning.

The phone was ringing. A woman's voice answered, "Good morning, this is the Animal Clinic. May I help you?"

Katrina replied, "Yes our family just got a puppy and would like to make an appointment for sometime next week to get his first year shots."

"The receptionist answered politely, Okay let me see, we can schedule the appointment next Wednesday eleven or we have three o'clock available?"

Katrina went over to the family calendar to look if she had the date and time free. "Yes I will take the eleven appointment time, what do I need to bring with us?" she asked.

"You will need to bring the puppy and a stool sample so we can get him on prevention for heartworm." the receptionist replied. Katrina wrote down the information on the small pad of paper so she could add the appointment to the calendar.

K.R. FISCHER

"Okay we will see you next week." She responded to the receptionist. "Does the puppy have a name yet, so that I can write him in our schedule?" the receptionist asked.

Katrina replies, "Yes, he does. His name is Peter and my name is Katrina Garrett."

"Is there a phone number where you can be reached just in case our office needs to change the appointment?" the receptionist asked.

"Yes it is 541-5656," Katrina Replied. Katrina looked around the corner to check on the two children playing in the other room. "Thank you is there anything else you need or questions you may have?" the receptionist asked.

"No that should do it," she answered. Then she hung up the phone, now she could go on and do the housework. Junior did not have preschool on Fridays so she had no errands to do and tomorrow the family would go see Dr. McDoodle to finish the necessary testing. She would ask Dean to do the errands at that time. Katrina picked up the rest of the kitchen. Rosa had stopped playing with her brother. Rosa came into the kitchen to see what she was doing.

"Mommy wet!" Rosa said. Katrina took Rosa into the bathroom but it was already too late to put her onto the potty chair. Rosa now needed to have a new pull-up on and a change of clothes. Katrina had a small storage tote in the bathroom will extra clothes for her and Junior along with baby wipes and pull-ups. She changed Rosa's clothes. They went into the other room where a basket of toys was spread out all over the floor. Katrina sat down on the floor to be with Rosa and Junior while they played.

"Mommy look at Peter he is playing with a sock." Junior stated. She had a pair of socks that one had a hole in and had gave it to Peter to play with until they went to the store to buy an actual dog chew toy. Peter was chewing away at the old sock.

"WAYNE IS STILL at school and will be home soon. Junior, why don't you go get your snow pants, boots, and coat on the hooks? This way Mommy can help you put them on to go outside and play in the snow." She said. Junior went into the bathroom used the potty chair and ran to get his outdoor gear off the hooks. "Here mommy!" he said with some excitement. Katrina began the task of putting on the snow pants. Peter had got up and was watching everyone. Rosa now was stirring and soon would be awake just in time for Katrina to get her snow suit on and then they could go outside. Katrina had put on a ski sweater over her medium built body and had put her long black hair up in a bun so that her beanie hat could cover her ears. It was not long before everyone was dresses warmly and they opened the garage to pull out a sled and bucket to play with out in the snow. Katrina put on a leash on Peter and then they were all outside playing in the snow. It had stopped snowing and the sun was bright today. They were building a snow fort before long she heard the school bus stop at the corner. Wayne was home from school and would want to play outside until dinner time. He came running down the incline to the back yard.

"Why don't you take your school bag and put it on the dining room table and then you can come outside to play," she stated. "Okay Mom and I will get the other bucket so I can help in building the snow fort." he replied. He was only gone for a few minutes before he came back outside and by Junior. They had built the fort waist high and now they wanted to build a snowman. It was time for mommy and Rosa to go in so she could start making dinner. She picked up a very wet and cold Rose then headed inside the house. The winter days seemed like that were dragging on and on. She made dinner that night and got the diaper bag ready for the next day. It was after dinner when she finished giving Rosa her bath and put her into a play pen. Next she would start Junior's bath water before cleaning up the kitchen.

"Get your pajamas out and lay them on your bed so when you are done with bath time you can get ready for bed". Everyone was tired after being outside earlier and was yawning. She was glad that they were tired and tonight would be an early bed time. The books that Junior and Wayne picked were their favorites for her to read and before she finished the first book they were asleep. Katrina took each one to their beds for the night. She finished picking up the house and put her pajama's on.

The phone rang and she answered it was Dean. "Hi Babe is everything alright? I was just going to bed so I can get up early in the morning." She stated in a lazy tone.

"No I was calling you to say goodnight and I would be working later than normal," He responded. "Oh, okay goodnight, I will see you in the morning," she said and then hung up the phone and went to bed.

The next morning Katrina and Rosa were the first ones up. She had put Rosa into the high chair and gave her a chopped banana. She packed the cooler with finger foods and juice boxes. She heard Dean in the shower and Junior had entered the kitchen.

"Mommy what's for breakfast?" he asked. "I have a fruit cup ready for you and a bowl of Sugarsnaps cereal," she replied. Katrina had stop giving the children a lot of sugary foods to help in the behavior category. Unfortunately it seemed to only help just a little. The rest of the family was now up and Katrina needed to get herself and Rosa ready to leave.

"Dean, can you finish getting the boys breakfast and dressed him to leave? I will put out their clothes to wear today so I can go and get ready to leave, too."

"Yes, sure," was all he said. Katrina took a quick shower and dressed in a pair of Lees and blouse. Dean was just finishing dressing Junior."

So how do I look?" she was waiting for an answer. He glanced up and answered her. "Fine I guess". He took Junior's hand and they walked toward the garage.

"Wayne it's time to get into the caravan. You can bring your little Thomas engine." She yelled up the stairs. "Did anyone take Peter outside to go to the bathroom?" No one answered her.

So she took the new leash that Dean had picked up on the way home. "Come here boy, here Peter! Peter!" she called in a loud voice. Peter came waddling in from the other room. She fastened his leash and took him outside to go to the bathroom and then brought him back inside. Katrina heard the caravan's horn honk several times. Dean had put all the children in the car and impatiently was waiting for her to come. He was getting ready to honk the horn when Katrina got in the front seat. They still had about an hour drive to Dr. McDoodle office for the rest of Junior's testing and evaluation. The sun was bright causing the snow to glisten against the bright blue sky. Katrina reached to turn on the radio. She glanced back to check on Rosa, Junior, and Wayne. Rosa was already asleep. Junior was looking out the window and Wayne was playing with his little cars.

"Mommy, how soon are we going to get there?" Junior was asking with his blanket next to him.

"We will be there in a while," she replied. Katrina had brought with her a magazine to look at to pass the time. She was flipping through it and looking at the recipes. When she finally looked up from the magazine and saw the city limit sign. They were close to the doctor's office. Katrina looked back to see that Rosa had woke up and was playing with a toy that Wayne had got from the diaper bag. They made a right turn and then a left hand turn into the parking lot of the building. Dean turned off the caravan and went around to the door. Wayne unbuckled his seatbelt and climbed out of the caravan.

"Wayne stay near the vehicle while Dad unbuckles your sister and brother," Katrina stated. Dean handed her the diaper bag and Rosa. She put Rosa down and grabbed her tiny hand. Katrina took Wayne and Rosa toward the office. Dean held Junior's hand and then locked up the caravan. They caught up with them as they were opening the door. Katrina let go of Rosa's hand so she could climb the stairs. They all made it upstairs to the waiting room. The receptionist handed her a clipboard to sign in and then she told Dr. McDoodle that they were there. Dr. McDoodle came out to say hello then asked Junior to follow him. "Once I am done testing and evaluating him I will send him out to get you. I will at that time need to see all of you in the conference room." Dr. Mc Doodle explained. Dean had left to make a phone call on his portable phone for the office they gave him so he could check on the main frame computer. Katrina was helping Rosa color in an animal coloring book. "Mr. and Mrs. Garrett, Rosa, and Wayne could you meet Junior and me in the back room?" Dr. McDoodle said calmly. Katrina took Rosa's hand and they all walked back to the room. Katrina felt like she was going to the principal's office when she was younger. They sat on a couch while Dr. Mc Doodle sat in a big leather chair. "I'm finished with all the testing and I will be giving you a prescription to help keep Junior on task. Now it is possible that I will need to adjust the dosage but for right now he should take it the days he goes to preschool," he explained.

Dr. Mc Doodle had put some building blocks on the table and puzzles for the children to play with while he talked to Katrina and Dean. Dr. McDoodle handed the prescription to her. "Sometimes during puberty they out grow it however, there a small percentage that don't he could have it when he becomes an adult. I have noticed that when Junior gets frustrated that the angry gets out of hand and he has an anger psychosis." Dr. McDoodle continued talking. "I also want you to schedule with one of our psychologist that works with children with ADD and psychosis. I believe he can help with Junior's anger issues and show him steps to handle it." Mentally Katrina knew that once they would leave the office Dean would show that he was disgusted and blame her about Junior. "Dr. McDoodle is there any counselors here today? Junior sometimes has problems with change and meeting new people." She asked quizzically. "Yes, Dr. James Willard is here in the office. Let me see if he has any clients right know and I will introduce your family to him." Dr. McDoodle stated. Dr. McDoodle left the room to check Dr. Willard's schedule. He came back into the room with Dr. Willard. "Dr. Willard this is Mr. and Mrs. Garrett, Wayne, Junior and Rosa. The patient is Junior, I have diagnosed him of having ADD and anger psychosis." "Good afternoon Dr.Willard, please call me Katrina. Junior please come over here I want you to meet Dr. Willard." Junior slowly came over to Katrina holding a puzzle piece. He wasn't happy about being interrupted in his play time. "Junior this is Dr. Willard he will be your counselor," Katrina stated. "Hi my name is Junior can I go finish playing." "Thank you Dr. Willard for taking your time," Dr. McDoodle replied. Dr. Willard left the room and Dr. McDoodle shut his office door. "I would like to see Junior in three or four months and you can make an appointment with the receptionist. Then you should make an appointment for Dr. Willard for next week. Rosa came over and wanted to sit on Dean's lap. He picked her up as they got ready to leave the office.

DEAN WAS VERY quiet through the visit. Katrina shook Dr. McDoodle's hand, "Thank you Dr. McDoodle for everything I will begin the prescription tomorrow and talk to the preschool on Monday. They left the office and Dean took the children to the caravan while Katrina scheduled the upcoming appointments.

Once she scheduled the appointments she went out to the caravan where Dean was waiting for her. She got into the caravan and buckled up for the ride home. "Dean you were very quiet while sitting in the consultation when Dr. McDoodle was explaining everything." She wanted to hear what Dean thought about everything.

"I am trying to absorb all the information Dr. McDoodle gave us today. I don't know what to think right now." he replied while driving along the county roads to get home. She now knew since the doctor's visit there was hope to help their son function in society. The psychiatrist and counselor appointments would be every couple of weeks then months for a very long time but she was ready for the challenge. She was hoping that her husband and family would be supportive in the long haul. The days went quickly to weeks then months and years as the family faced new challenges. The puppy Peter grew into a healthy large beagle along with bonding with the oldest son.

WAYNE AND JUNIOR attended the neighborhood elementary school. Rosa attended a preschool for two years before going to the same elementary school her brothers attended. The children tried several different extracurricular activities to find out what they enjoyed before joining the team. Katrina would end up taking care of the family dog especially when the children were busy doing their things. Katrina kept busy with her children's activities but also found some hobbies of her own. Although most of the time she was taking the children to their dance class, baseball games, hockey games, ice skating lessons, bowling, or programs at the school. She still was able to do the interior decorating of the new house and an annually flower garden outside. Katrina and Dean had found that they were comfortable with their lifestyle. Junior's ADD and anger psychosis was under control. The hope of him having a semi-normal school life was attained through time management and medication. It was time for her to do more things she enjoyed with all of her children now in school all day. She did more volunteer work for local non-profit organizations. One day she thought it was time to take some continuing education adult classes at the community college and finish getting her associate or bachelor degree.

"Hi Babe, how was your day at the office?" she looked up from pouring each of them a glass of a fruity Rose dinner wine."

"It was fine and just feels that it is taking longer to get home since the beginning of the month with all the road construction being done on the major highways." He responded with a sigh. "Can you please finish serving our dinner while I go and check on the children in the play room?"

I will put a Disney movie in for them to watch and if it is finished I want to begin another one so we can eat and talk." Katrina stated as she walked out of the dining area.

Katrina entered the playroom and the movie looked as if it finished a time ago but the children had found different building toys in the toy chest and was content. She went back to the dining area to join Dean for dinner. No longer did she sit down and had a few bites of her meal.

She heard Rosa yell, "That is not fair, and I had it first and quite knocking my doll house down!" Katrina quickly got up from the dining room table to take care of the squabble the children were apparently having in the other room. She got there just in time before Rosa started crying. She took Rosa over to where more blocks were and comforted her until she stopped crying.

She would have to talk to Dean about her going back to work part-time and the upcoming family vacation. Every year the family went on vacation to see relatives but also to visit historical sites. Last year the family vacation was to visit Katrina's younger sister Martha and her family in Florida. Wayne, Junior, and Rosa were old enough to enjoy the rides, thrills and fun at Walt Disney World. Katrina felt a little like a child because it was also the first time she had been to Walt Disney World and she wanted a picture of herself with Mickey Mouse. This year their vacation was to visit family in Virginia then go to Gettysburg then drive to the Washington D. C. area to see the monuments, Library of Congress, George Washington's house and visit Arlington Cemetery. The whole vacation was to take almost three weeks with driving time. They would leave at the end of July and return by the week of the county fair. Then Katrina would have to register the two boys in the new middle school and take them school shopping. She would take Rosa on a separate school shopping day since her registration was done before summer vacation. Wayne and Junior had their own friends that came to the house on weekends to play the latest in game system games or computer games. When they were hanging out with their friends at numerous hockey games at the park district and figure skating programs during the school year took up a lot of their time.

Katrina had helped Rosa get ready for the first day of school. She had brushed Rosa's strawberry blonde hair and put it into pigtails. "Mom, why do I have to take all this with me to school today?" said Rosa. "Yes this list is what came with all the new school year papers in the mail. I will drive you to school so that you won't have to carry the back pack." she replied. Wayne and Junior had already left on the middle school bus with another new boy. The new boy lived in the newly built house kiddy corner from them. The family moved in while they were on vacation. There was a boy around Wayne and Junior's age along with a girl around Rosa's age. Katrina was happy that they had neighbors with children. Unfortunately, year's later justice would be what Katrina wanted so badly so that their family would heal and find that hope was still a long road to travel. Justice as a nation and as a family would be something that their family would need to address one event at a time.

It was a weekday Dean had left a little earlier to go to work because his car needed an oil change. Junior and Rosa were already at school. Katrina had to take Wayne to the dentist for his six month cleaning and check up. She waited in the waiting room while Wayne was with the dentist and technician for a good twenty minutes. She was reading an article in one of their magazines with the television set on a local station. The volume was low just as white noise, but Katrina for some reason just looked up to see that the news was showing a commercial airplane hitting one of the Twin Towers in New York City. She dropped the magazine onto the floor as she watch the news there was a bright flash on the television and the other tower looked like it was hit too.

Katrina turned the volume up and told the receptionist to look at the television. "Oh my God!" she screamed.

The receptionist went back to her desk and was shaking her head from side to side. The technician came out to get Katrina so that she could go back to the room where Wayne was sitting with the dentist. When she got back there they also had the news on and had seen what Katrina saw a few minutes ago. The news showed the scenes in downtown New York City as the first tower collapsed and then the second. The news people that were live showed the chaos on the streets. Once the dentist appointment was over and she was driving Wayne back to the middle school.

"Mom was the news on television right about it, was it really a terrorist attack that hit the Twin Towers?" Wayne was chattering about the news all the way to the middle school. Katrina was shocked about what the news was on the radio that it was a terrorist attack on American soil.

K.R. FISCHER

The news reported that two more commercial airplanes went down; one went down at the Pentagon in Washington D.C. and another in a farm field somewhere in Pennsylvania. All Katrina wanted to do was to sign, Wayne in at the school office and she went straight home to call her younger sister. Katrina was just outside the middle school when the loud speaker was requesting all teachers to turn on their televisions in their classrooms and discuss with students what was currently happening in our country. Katrina did not know what to feel as she started up her caravan to drive home. She pulled the van into the garage and turned on the television the live news was giving the count of the dead so far. Katrina picked up the telephone to call her sister in Florida to see if her husband was alright. Her sister's husband was working for a major credit card company with their main office being near the Twin Towers. She was hoping that this time he was still in Florida. The phone rang several times before her sister Martha picked up. She took a few deep breathes before asking,

"Hi sis, did you see the news this morning about the Twin Towers? Did Bailey have to go to work in New York City this week by chance?" she could tell by the hesitation that Martha was a little bothered by the questions. Martha replied, "Why are you asking about Bailey working from home this week. Yes, I heard about the Twin Towers and I still cannot believe it." Katrina gave a sigh of relieve. "I am happy that he is safe and since I have you on the phone, how are my nephew's Colton and Blade doing? "Colton likes being the big brother and Blade is now crawling," Martha stated calmly. "Well I called to make sure everyone is fine and I am happy to hear that you guys are and I will talk you again soon. Have a good day sis. Give each of the boys a bunch of hugs and kisses from their Auntie." Martha replied.

I will and you have a good day too again thanks for calling about all us. Good-bye!" they both hung up the phones. Katrina sat in the living room on the couch to watch more of the news reports. She walked across the street to see if the neighbor had heard about what had happened earlier in the day. She rang the door bell and then knocked but the neighbor was not at home so she walked back to her house.

She called Dean, "Hi babe, did you see the news reports today?" She asked.

Dean answered, "Yes I did the company is on high alert so I cannot be on the phone I will be late tonight and we will talk when I come home later." The children would be home from school soon and she had to get herself together before then. The president was going to address the nation and send troops to the Middle East to combat the threat of terrorism. She went down stairs to get the next load of laundry started when she heard the front door open.

Junior screaming, "Mom where are you?" "Mom, mom are you here!" as Wayne was seeking for a response.

"Boys I will be there in just a minute I'm just downstairs," She had both hands on the clothes basket that she was bringing up the stairs. She was short winded as she cleared the top of the last stairs. "okay boys why don't you sit at the dining room table and start your homework. While I put this in my bedroom to put away later and I will make a healthy snack for everyone." She heard the door and Rosa was home from school now too.

"Mommy I heard that bad men today hurt a lot of people, is this true?" Rosa said in a confused state." Katrina knew that she had to answer but in a delicate and sensible way.

"Yes, Rosa bad things happened today and during dinner we can talk about what happened." "Do you have any homework tonight?" Rosa gave her mom a sigh and replied, "Yes I have spelling words and a math work sheet." The children were busy with their homework and afternoon snack. It was time to start preparing dinner, but her stomach was still upset and queasy from the news broadcast of earlier in the day. She had not been able to eat except for a piece of toast and some crackers. The television was off temporary but she would need to see the late news after the children went to bed for the night. Wayne and Junior were done with their homework. Wayne went to play one of the strategy games for the gaming systems and Junior followed him with one of the extra controllers. Rosa finished shortly after that but she had the chore to set the table tonight and then wash up for dinner. They all ate dinner in silence Katrina couldn't stand it.

"Okay what is going on as she asked her children?" They all looked at one another.

Wayne decided to start, "Mom why would anyone want to hurt so many people and here in the United States?"

"I don't know;" was all she could respond with at that moment. "What did the teachers at school have to say?" she waited to see which one would reply to the question.

Rosa was still very quiet compared to her chattering self especially at dinner time. She could see something was disturbing her daughter internally but did not know exactly what.

"The teacher's talked about the Middle East history and about the terrorist group called Al-Qaeda and that we were to have a discussion in our history class." Wayne said.

"I heard that the president was going to address the nation on television and our government would be sending military troops to stop them from doing his again to our country," was Junior's response.

"Well boys if you are done eating will you please rinse off your dishes and put them in the sink," Katrina looked over at Rosa where she was playing with her food.

"What's wrong Rosa? You have hardly eaten any of your dinner tonight." Rosa just stared at her with a blank face. "Do you want to talk about it later?" she asked and Rosa responded with a shake of her head and left the dinner table.

Katrina turned on the television just in time to hear the president come on to address the nation about what was going to be done with the terrorist attacks on United States soil. Katrina was still saddened by the loss of life but she was also angry for the people that used the commercial airplanes as a fueled bomb.

The president was definitely sending troops to look for all the terrorism cells throughout the Middle East and there would be stricter regulations for the nation's airports. The event would change everyone's life because not only did Katrina and other American citizens want justice for what these terrorist groups did to so many innocent people on the commercial airplanes but for those individuals that were working in the Twin Towers, the Pentagon, the Firemen that were in harm's way when the Towers collapsed. The threat that it might happen again would be constantly on everyone's mind on a day-to-day basis. The next part the news program showed the Pentagon and the plane still inside the building. Katrina's eyes swelled up with tears and then she noticed her daughter pointing at the television.

"Mommy we were just there visiting right before school started." She was saying with some hesitations as she tried not to cry.

Then she ran out of the room into her and Dean's bedroom climbed into the bed then grabbed the blanket to cover her head. Katrina then knew that Rosa not only remembers their last vacation but that the family had been at the corner with the jumbo commercial airplane had gone into the Pentagon building. Katrina told the boys to get ready for bed and to make sure they brushed their teeth.

"Mom we won't forget to brush our teeth," came from the other room with Wayne and Junior said in unison. Katrina told Rosa to stay there while she went to say goodnight to both boys. She went to Wayne's room first to tuck him and say goodnight.

"Goodnight and don't let the bed bugs bite. I love you." She said as she turned off the light.

Wayne said quietly, "I love you too Mom."

She was already to Junior's room to see he had already gone to sleep. She pulled up the covers and kissed his forehead. On the way back to her bedroom she checked to make sure the front door was locked, the television was turned off and all the lights. Then she stopped at Rosa's bedroom to get her a nightgown to wear and her favorite stuffed animal. When she got to her room Rosa had curled up on Dean's side of the bed and was almost asleep. Katrina got ready for bed and sat next to Rosa. She pulled off her dirty day clothes and dressed her for bed.

"Rosa you can sleep with Mommy and Daddy tonight. You do know Mommy and Daddy would never let anything happen to you." "We both love you very much." Was all she could say as she held her daughter until she was completely a sleep?

She knew that when Dean did finally come home from work, he would carry their daughter into her own room and her own bed. She lay next to Rosa and before long they were both sound to sleep. The next several months every time Rosa heard any type of plane go over their house she would run and say,

"Mommy those bad men are going to do it again they are going to crash into the houses."

It would be a year later before Rosa would actually sleep back in her own bed and her own room. The safety at the airports around the United

27

States had stricter policies and regulations in hopes to stop any more terrorist attacks on American soil. All she knew that the people or group that did this needed to be brought to justice.

The following year Katrina and Rosa needed to move on with their lives. The best way sometimes is to face their fears and it no better to do it when they decided to go to Louisiana for the Fourth of July week. This year Floyd's family was hosting the reunion just north of Baton Rouge for the weekend. Junior and Dean would be gone that same week too, but they were going to a summer camp in the upper part of Wisconsin. Katrina and Rosa were flying out the following Monday from an International air port to New Orleans. Wayne was coming with Katrina's parents and staying at the Louisiana State Park in their 40 foot motor home. Katrina had not been back to Louisiana since she was in college. The memories of that year were coming back only too vividly. One day she might be able to tell Wayne, Junior, or Rosa the story. They would get in to New Orleans late morning at the French Quarters where the hotel they were staying and rent a car. They were checking in at the front desk.

"Mame here is the room key you requested for room number 911 the elevator is just over there!"

She took the key from the clerk. "Thank you Henrietta," she said. Rosa and she took their luggage up to their room.

"Rosa, why don't you go ahead and put your pack back on the table and then go put on your swimsuit on so we can take a quick swim before dinner." She said while putting her own one piece swimsuit on with a wrap. She wanted to relax a bit before going to the family reunion tomorrow. They would go out to dinner and walk around to discover what else they were going to do as there adventure was to begin after the reunion. It wasn't that she did not want to be with family but she wanted Rosa to see things that she would never see before. Rosa and she went up on the next floor to the pool. She had brought a magazine to read and had picked up several pamphlets of sightseeing tours.

She looked over them and decided that she would call one of the alligator tours and the plantation tours to see about the cost first thing in the morning. Rosa enjoyed being able to swim.

"Mom looks what I can do!" Rosa said as she went under the water to do a handstand.

Katrina looked up and watched her daughter do her aquatics and then looked at her watch.

They had already been at the pool for almost two hours and she was getting hungry. "Rosa it's time to get out of the pool and dry off so we can go out to dinner!"

"Mom do I have too just a little bit more time, please" Rosa said.

"Okay, fifteen more minutes and that's all" she replied. She set her watch for fifteen more minutes and watched her daughter swim. "Okay Rosa time is up!" Rosa did not argue about more time she got out of the pool then sat beside her for a few minutes.

"I have some really neat things to show you what I have planned after we see nana and papa tomorrow." Katrina got up from the chase lounge and Rosa followed her to the elevator.

"Mom what are we going to for dinner I'm hungry?" Rosa stated in a whinny voice.

"Well we need to get dressed remember to wear one of your nice short outfits and we will ask the front desk clerk if they have any suggestions for a good restaurant to eat at." They changed into summer clothes even when the sun went down it were still in the mid 80's and very humid outside.

The desk clerk was no longer Henrietta it was a young man. "Maybe you can help us sir we are wondering where a good restaurant is for dinner tonight do you have any suggestions."

The young man looked up from the computer. "There are a few restaurants in walking distance, but my favorite is on the corner about a block from here that serves excellent Louisiana crawfish." He replied.

Katrina thanked the young man then her and Rosa began to walk along the bricked street.

"Mom can we stop in here, I want to buy one of those mask for a souvenir." Katrina looked at the shop and then decides that why not it might be closed on the way back from dinner. They went into the Mardi Gras shop to purchase one of the masks. Then went on their walk toward the area where the clerk had told them about and there was a figurine in front of the door of a man with a saxophone.

"Mom is this it?" "Yes I believe." As they both went into the quaint restaurant and waited for the maître d' to seat them.

"Good evening ladies I have a table over there by the window," My name is Pierre and your waiter tonight will be Sean."

"Thank you and they both began to look at the menu. She wanted to try their jambalaya and a wine.

"I don't see anything I would like mom they don't have grilled cheese or French fries?" Sean, the waiter was there to take their order. "I was wandering my daughter would like a grilled cheese sandwich and French fries is there any way that the chef can make it?"

"I will check but I'm pretty sure that it won't be a problem but I will go and ask him." He was back to their table quickly. "The chef said it was no problem." Sean said.

"Then I would like to order a grilled cheese sandwich, an order of French fries, and a root beer. I would also like a glass of your house wine with a jambalaya and house salad." Katrina placed the order.

The small restaurant was decorated in honor of jazz musicians. There was photos of Jazz musician on the walls and a street musician was somewhere outside because you could hear him play a mixture of the Blues and Jazz. Their dinner was good but of course a little too spicy than what she was used to but she knew that was a possibility when she order dinner. They finished dinner and began walking back to the hotel Katrina did not want her and Rosa outside after dark because of the known Voodoo history and stories.

They would get a good night s sleep and get up the next morning to drive over to the State Park where the family had rented a cabin. Rosa would be able to meet for the first time relatives. They would visit and stay one night in the cabin with other family members. Nana and Papa were there from New Mexico along with Papa's sisters'. Katrina was visiting with her first cousins and their families. Many of them had not seen each other in many years so there was a lot of catching up to do. There was plenty of food including some Cajun dishes and of course Jambalaya to eat. Papa started to play a card game with Rosa and Charlotte. Uncle Charlie had finished eating and was the official auctioneer for the family. There were plenty of unusual items on the auctioneer table for everyone to bid on. Uncle Charlie got up in the front of the room by the table.

"Alright everyone did you get enough to eat if you didn't then it's your own fault.

We will start at a dollar anyone two dollars?" The bidding was in full swing with the youngest bidding on a toy to a gift card for a bed and breakfast. The money from the auction would be given to the next family that would host the reunion the following year. The auction was over and everyone paid what they owed for the trinkets that they had bought. Katrina needed to go for a walk to stretch her legs.

"Rosa, do you want to go for a walk along the trail with us?"

"Papa I will be right back I want to go with my mom and the rest along the trail." Rosa said. They were following one of men that lived down here and married to one of Katrina's cousins'. "Be careful there is water moccasins near-by," was all he said.

Rosa got in front of her but stayed close. Katrina happened to just look up and saw a large black coil in the tree. "Rosa be careful," as she pointed in the tree.

"Mom what was that? It is big and ugly!" "I believe you can say it was a very big snake and probably a water moccasin." She said in a lower voice so that it would not scare the rest of the younger children. They went back on a different trail not to bother the big snack and get to the cabin.

Rosa joined back into the card game until it was time to go into the girl's side of the cabin and sleep on bunk beds. The next morning some of the relative would be leaving after breakfast and they would begin their adventure of exploring the swamps and history of Louisiana.

Rosa and I went on an alligator tour boat to see them in the wild the next day. The tour guide introduces himself as Horace but everyone called him Gatorman. He had a baby one as a pet to give everyone a chance to touch and even hold it.

"Can I hold it Mom, please?" Rosa looked at her.

"Yes remember it is a baby," she said with a smile. Once the tour guide gave the group information about the alligators and the history of the area the boat had left the dock. They were going into the bayou and swamp.

"Please don't hang over the railing around the edge of the boat or your hands! The railing is there for your protection from the alligators this is their territory." Gatorman stated. He slowed the boats motor. "Will everyone take a look over to the right of the boat you will see them sunning themselves which also makes them slower to move?" The next thing we saw was Gatorman reaching inside a big plastic bucket and pulling out raw chicken.

Rosa gave a stared look. "Mommy what is he getting ready to do?"

"I think he is getting ready to feed some of them." All of a sudden an alligator actually jumped out of the water to grab the chicken.

"Mom...my!" was all Rosa could voice. They looked into the water there several alligators of different sizes waiting to see if more food was going to become available. Gatorman pulled out two more chickens from the bucket.

"Now when I drop this one in, you will see how the bigger one will get the food and swallow it in one gulp!"

Rosa raised her hand. "Have you ever lost a finger or part of your hand when you were feeding them?" Gatorman looked at Rosa,

"Yes, I have lost my whole arm." Then everyone started to laugh as a fake hand came out of the jacket. "Taking all seriousness I have had a few fingers taking off and he held up his hand where once two fingers had been and now where only knobs. I have the utmost respect for these creatures. I have had a few close calls and I am thankful that nothing serious has been bitten off." They continued the tour watching the side where there were more alligators. There were two that seemed to be following the tour boat. Many of the passengers had become silent after Gatorman showed his missing fingers.

"Is there any other questions, I will be heading back to the dock." The rest of the ride was quiet and when Gatorman had pulled the boat up next to the dock. They had to drive back to the hotel tonight and Katrina had made reservations on the following day to visit a southern plantation that was hosting a mother and daughter luncheon. They were there the entire afternoon and then back to the hotel. The trip worked like Katrina was hoping because Rosa was no longer having issues about the commercial airplanes. There trip had gone by quickly and it was time to head home. Dean was picking them up from the airport after eight o'clock p.m.

Hi Honey, how was the drive into the airport?"

"The traffic had died down since rush hour we should be home in just over a hour." he continued. "I had a rough day at the office sometimes I just don't understand why people cannot just follow simple instructions."

She was trying to listen to him but she was tired after their flight and was anxious to get home. "Well, I'm sure that you are just being misunderstood and things will work out. How were the boys at the week of camp?"

"The camp was fine all week and only one day it rained," he said.

Dean turned on the radio and before long she was able to drift off to sleep. She woke up when she heard the trunk close to Dean's work car. He carried Rosa into her bedroom leaving on the clothes she wore and tucked into bed. He had already carried the suitcases into the house. She changed quickly into a nightshirt and climbed into their bed. She would worry about unpacking tomorrow. The boys had stayed with Katrina and Dean's friends Bobby Joe and her husband Paul; while Dean was at work that day. She would pick them up later the next morning and have a short visit with her best friend.

Bobby Joe also had three children; two boys and a girl. Bobby Jo's oldest Patrick was only a year older than Wayne. Then Junior was just a year older than Randall. Her daughter Danaka was a year older than Rosa. The families did a lot of barbeques during the summer, went to activities together, and had game night and popcorn during the snowy winter months. Bobby Jo was a few years older than Katrina and had a bachelor degree in chemistry. Katrina admired Bobby Jo because she had finished her college education and became a stay at home mom. Bobby Jo was taller than Katrina, she had brown eyes, her dark brown hair was done in a pixie style, and she reminded others of a scientist or librarian with the conservative nature. Katrina thought that Bobby Jo had a heart of gold because she was always volunteering at one of the many nonprofit organizations. Her husband Paul worked the night shift at one of the state disability homes. Paul was towering over six feet, his natural curly black hair was thinning at the top and his demeanor reminded you of a person that could joke around with close friends. He and Dean enjoyed playing around with broken computers when they got together during family get-togethers. Patrick looked a lot like his dad Paul just a smaller version while Randall was more athletic and enjoyed computer games. Danaka was a brunette that had it up in a pony tail and was definitely a tom-boy just like Rosa. They would rather go fishing together or catch fireflies than play with dolls. Bobby Jo and she would have play dates until the girls were old enough to go to school. Then the boys were in Boy Scouts and the girls were in Girl Scouts together. Bobby Jo was a Girl Scout Leader and a den mother. Katrina was an assistant in Girl Scouts while she was a committee chair in the Cub Scouts. The training and meetings kept them busy along with regularly helping their children with school work. Then Randall and Danaka began to go to Karate lessons during the week. While Junior was interested in the park district hockey and Rosa began ice skating lessons. Rosa began to excel with the lessons and soon was beginning to go to figure skating competitions. Although the families seemed to grow apart they still managed to get together a couple of times during the summer months and during the Christmas holidays. It was the holidays and Bobby Jo along with Patrick, Randall and Rosa were coming over to celebrate New Year's Eve.

"Come on in Bobby Jo, I'm in the kitchen fixing snacks for the boys," she said. "Patrick and Randall go ahead a go downstairs into the family room where Wayne and Junior are playing one of the new games they got for Christmas on the Atari System."

"Where is Rosa?" Danaka was taking off her coat as she went toward Rosa's bed room.

She replied, "Danaka I'm in here with my new stuffed animals and we are at the doctor's." Danaka had a gift bag for Rosa.

"Hey Mommy, look what Danaka brought me!" as she came into the kitchen to show her that it was a very large stuffed puppy.

"That was very nice of you Danaka to get Rosa a Christmas gift."

"Rosa why don't you go and get Danaka's gift under the Christmas tree for her to open, before telling the boys to come up to eat a snack. This way then we can exchange gifts."

"Here is my gift for you Bobby Jo and the tin of popcorn is for the family," she said while pouring another cup of tea. "Katrina it matches the other angel I have sitting on our fireplace mantel, it's beautiful."

Bobby Jo handed her a small package she opened it to see a small friendship charm bracelet. She gave Bobby Jo a hug just as all the children came into the kitchen for their snacks.

"Thank you Bobby Jo for such a beautiful gift," was all she said. It was just a little after 10 p.m. and she needed to put on the television for the countdown to the New Year. She called all the children so they could participate in the ringing in the New Year by counting backwards and watching the ball fall at Times Square in New York City.

It was hard to believe that the year went by so quickly and no one knew what the upcoming year would bring them. Situations would happen that Katrina would need more than hope to keep her family together. She was sure that the New Year would be full of surprises and plenty of challenges.

ONCE SPRING ARRIVED and the birds were chirping in the early morning hours when she noticed that a moving van was across the street. The new neighbors were moving in and she would go later in the week to introduce herself.

It was a Thursday afternoon and Katrina walked across the road to introduce herself to the new neighbors. She had a small welcome gift of a combination of spring flower bulbs and a watering can. She rang the door bell a women answered the door. She was around the same age of Katrina. The women had dark long black hair and she wore a pair of thick glasses on a large nose. She was taller than Katrina by at least a good five inches and had an hour glass figure.

"Good afternoon, I am your neighbor; I live across the street from you. My name is Katrina Garrett. I want to welcome you and your family to our neighborhood. I have a welcome gift bag for you; I thought you might want to plant some spring bulbs this coming fall."

"Thank you Katrina, my name is Prudence Hallow, but everyone calls me by my nickname Prue. Why don't you come in for a visit, I am still unpacking some boxes in the kitchen. I was wandering how long have you lived in this area."

"My husband, kids and I moved out here just over six years ago and love the community." Katrina replied.

"Our family used to live in the suburbs of the city and lived in an apartment. This is the first time we actually have owned a house. My daughter Cassandra will start first grade in the fall. My son Pete will be in the third grade. My husband Tobi has not found work out here so he is still working part time in the apartment complex where we use to live.

Katrina never saw Tobi except at night when he got home from work. Pete played with Junior after school. Tobi had talked to Dean about the boy's possible playing junior league hockey. Tobi had asked Dean if Pete could ride with Junior to the ice arena for practices.

"I have a daughter that will start a kindergarten and first grade program in the fall. She still is behind when it comes to comprehending her reading. My two boys are older and two years apart. Hopefully, this summer our families can get together for a few cookouts and other community festivities."

"That sounds great Katrina!" Prue finished putting the last of the dishes in the cabinet and emptied another packing box.

"Well I need to get home before my children get home from school. I still have a few things I need to finish up around the house. By the way Prue if there is anything you need or information about community happenings just gives me a call. Do you have a piece of paper and I will give you our phone number." Katrina wanted Prue to know that she was there for her.

Prue found an old envelope and a pen, and then handed it to Katrina. Then she wrote on another scrap piece of paper their new phone number. Katrina and Prue Hallow became friends right from the start. It was easy to become friends since Prue and her family moved in next door. Prue had a daughter Cassandra that was the same age of Katrina's daughter Rosa. Prue also had a son Pete that was a year younger than Katrina's son Junior. The children played together all the time except when her children went to extracurricular outings throughout the week. Cassandra and Rosa became the best of friends along with being together most of the time.

Then the truth of who Prue really was would emerge its ugly face on one hot summer day during an unusual conversation she had with Katrina. She had her doubts since she had heard her daughter talking with Cassandra on the phone a few weeks ago. While the girls were talking about school and Cassandra's mother who apparently had been snooping around her bedroom.

Rosa had replied "Why do moms think it is alright to snoop in our things when we cannot snoop in their belongings."

"I get into trouble even when I go into their room, "said Cassandra.

"Well I better go my mom just came into the room. I will see you tomorrow at the bus stop," said Rosa. She hung up the phone and skipped down the hallway.

The next morning Rosa was at the table eating her breakfast and getting ready to leave for the bus stop. She was wearing a short outfit and her hair in braids today.

"Mom will I need a jacket for school today?"

"Will you be picking me up from school today?"

"No Rosa you will be riding the bus home today and I will be picking you up tomorrow from school. You will need your sweater Rosa this morning but by the time you are on your way home it will be in the low 70's," she replied.

"See you later mom!" As Rosa went out the door and began skipping up to the bus stop.

While the children were in school, Katrina grabbed her craft tote and went over to Prue's house to work on the project for the upcoming spring craft fair. They only had a few weeks to finish for the craft fair which is in two weeks. Once the craft fair was over then it would be Memorial Day weekend which was considered to be the kick-off to summer. When she got together with Prue they would discuss their children and their spouses. She could tell that Prue was unhappy with her life and she needed the craft fair to help with extras in their household budget.

"Hypothetically Katrina what would you do if Rosa had been assaulted by someone you knew?"

She had been caught off guard by the question from Prue and at first was not sure how to answer it. She sat for a few minutes to thank about such a strange question to be asked by her close friend.

"I guess I would first talk with the parent or parents about the incidence so they could talk with their child." She answered with hesitation. "Why are asking?"

"Well I was in Cassandra's room and I found her diary. So, I began to read some of what she had written. I was bothered by a few sentences that she wrote and I am not sure what I should do." As Prue said this Katrina could tell that whatever she had read really upset her friend.

"So have you talked with the parent or parents? Or did you ask Cassandra about it?" stated Katrina.

"I did not say anything to Cassandra because I don't think I was supposed to read her diary." Prue looked at Katrina and then the room seemed considerable quiet all of a sudden. She was unsure why Prue was asking such an unusual question. She knew from past conversations that Prue was thinking about suing where she had worked a few months ago. Furthermore, she had asked Katrina if she knew of any good attorneys in the area. Katrina had another friend that worked in the town's attorney office as a personal secretary. Katrina had given Prue a few names that might help her and not cost a lot for her to hire to take the case.

Katrina glanced up to check the digital clock on the DVD player to see what the time was so that she would be home before the children arrived home from school. They both began the task of picking up and putting their homemade items that they would be selling in a large tote.

"Are we still planning to get together twice next week to complete making of the afghans' and to make the signs for the fair," She wanted to know.

"Yes, but I will need to go to a doctor appointment on one of the days so can we move it to Thursday. By the way do you know any attorney's that take cases dealing with civil suits?" Prue asked again with some hesitation.

Katrina arrived home just in time before the bus dropped off their children at the corner of the road. She had to look on the refrigerator to look at the family calendar about next Thursday. For some reason she had that day etched in for something else going on when it came to her. That was the day she would be going with her friend Bobby Jo to an end of the year banquet. She would call Prue in the morning after the children went to school and see if she could come over on Friday morning instead. Bobby Jo and Katrina had been best friends for a long time so she knew that going to the banquet would be a big deal so she would need Bobby Jo to pick her up that evening.

KATRINA BEGUN TO plan for Rosa's upcoming ninth birthday party before school was out for summer break.

"Mom can I invite some of my girl friends from school to come to my birthday party?" her daughter gave her a long list.

"Why don't we work on the birthday guest list after you do your homework and we have ate dinner," she answered.

Rosa sat down at the table and got out her spelling worksheets. Her brothers had also sat down at the table to do their homework. Katrina began the task of preparing dinner.

"Mom can you give me my spelling words and I will spell them out loud."

"Mom I am done with my homework can I go and play a video game until dinner is ready," said Junior.

"Do you want me to look over the work, Junior? Or are you sure about it being ready for class tomorrow," she usually checked Junior's homework because he had a tendency to skip sections without realizing that he did it. Wayne placed his homework in his book bag and went to his room to do an essay for English on his computer.

"Okay Rosa, are you ready for me to give you the spelling quiz?" She took the spelling list over to the counter by the stove while she kept an eye on the egg noodles cooking.

"Number one is the spelling word change. I will change my clothes when I get home from school today." Katrina read the spelling words one at a time, and then placed them into a sentence a total of ten different times.

"Okay Rosa, now go and wash up for dinner and I will check these in a few minutes," she commented. As she finished putting the salad onto the table along with egg noodles casserole on everyone's plate. "Junior! Rosa! Wayne! Dinner is ready!" She called from the kitchen table.

"Just a minute mom I need to finish this level then I can save the game," replied Junior.

"Just a few more minutes Junior is all you do have because then your dinner will be cold," was her response. Rosa sat down in her chair to eat dinner then Junior came and sat down at the end of the table. Shortly following was Wayne and he sat down next to his younger brother.

"Boy mom I am hungry, do I have to eat any salad? May I have some raw cut carrots instead?" Junior began playing with some of his food on his plate.

"I don't see why not. Do you want some carrots cut up too Rosa? Wayne?

"Yes please and thank you." All three children answered in unison.

Shortly after cleaning up after dinner and wiping off the table. Rosa and Katrina sat down at the table to begin making out the birthday party invites. They were inviting fifteen girls to come along with staying overnight for a girl slumber party. Katrina would order a few large pepperoni pizzas from the local Pizzeria and then the girls could watch a Disney movie on the big screen television in the main living room.

All the birthday invitations were finished and Rosa placed them in her school back pack to take them to school tomorrow to hand out to all her girl friends.

The next day Katrina had woke up early for some reason but the alarm went off in the boy's room. She could hear both of them getting ready for school while, Rosa came out of her room into hers.

"Mom do you know where my other sandal like this one?" Rosa held up a brown sandal to show her.

"No, I don't know why you didn't wear your tennis shoes instead." She answered.

The children finished their breakfast quickly, and then left for the school bus stop. Katrina again looked up more attorneys' that might help Prue in her civil suit. The phone numbers were local and one of the attorney's came highly recommended by another of Katrina's friend. Her friends Samantha was the secretary in a local attorney's office she had gave her another list of attorney's that were taking new clients.

She called Prue with the information, "I need to change next week's date of getting together to Friday instead of Thursday. I also have some more attorneys' that you might want to call about taking the civil suit." Katrina said.

"Thank you Katrina I have called several from the first list and you really have helped me." Was all Prue could say at that time.

"I see no problem next Friday, can you come around 10:30 because my prescription should be out of my system and I will be alert to work on the remaining section of the red afghan. Thanks again, I hope that I can get one of these attorney's to take my case. My husband's work hours were cut again and I cannot work since I fell at work months ago. Katrina, I really need to go so I can call some of these attorneys' and maybe schedule a few appointments in the next few weeks, Good-bye" as Prue hung up the phone.

"Good-bye Prue and have a nice day. I will talk with you if anything else changes." she said and hung up the phone.

It was finally Thursday and Katrina would need to remind Dean that he needed to be home early tonight because Bobby Jo was picking her up for the annual banquet. Wayne would help with getting dinner ready tonight. On the other hand Cassandra and Rosa stayed outside playing basketball in the driveway.

"Wayne can you please butter the bread so we can make toast in oven to go with dinner. I will also need you to watch the spaghetti noodles while I to take a quick shower and get dressed for the banquet tonight."

"Okay mom and is there anything else you need me to do?" Wayne was putting butter on the bread out of the refrigerator.

"No I don't think so," she replied. Then she walked to the master bedroom and bathroom in the back of the house. Katrina shortly just came out of her bedroom dressed in a pair of navy dress pants and a beige blouse. She walked to the front door to call Rosa to wash up and that it was time to eat dinner.

"Cassandra, it is time for you to go home while my children eat dinner and then they will need to stay inside until their dad gets home from work. Maybe once he gets home then Rosa can come back outside to play but that will be up to her dad." Katrina stated to Cassandra.

Rosa waved to Cassandra and yelled to her friend, "See you later okay?" While she came into the house and she watched her friend Cassandra cross the street to her own driveway.

Wayne, Junior and Rosa sat down in their chairs at the table to eat their dinner.

"Wayne and you both need to clear the table and put the dishes into the sink so when I get home later tonight I can clean up the kitchen. I also need all of you to make sure that all of your homework is done and you are in bed at the regular time, because tomorrow is still a school day." She kissed the children goodbye as her friend Bobby Jo began beeping the horn. When she called Dean that afternoon she also reminded him about the children's bedtime.

"Beep, Beep!" "Okay children, Bobby Jo is here and I am leaving, your dad will be here shortly. I should be home after your dad puts you to bed." Katrina made sure the front door locked behind her. Then she got into Bobby Jo's little economy car.

Katrina came home as the news came onto the television. Dean had finished cleaning up the kitchen and was already in their bed watching the late night news.

"So how was the banquet?" he asked.

"The banquet went fine, Bobby Jo received an award for leadership," she changed into her spring flower nightgown and climbed into bed next to her husband.

FRIDAY, MAY 9TH was Mother's Day weekend and Katrina had asked for a weekend of solitude by going to a town along the Mississippi River and staying in a bed and breakfast until Sunday evening. She would go over to Prue's house in the morning to work on the crafts and then be home by noon to eat lunch and pack an overnight bag so she would be able to leave before the children came home from school. She would go over at 10:30 like they had planned but leave earlier. She could hardly believe that it was Friday already with the sun coming through the front window into the living room. It looked like the weekend was going to have warm temperatures and a chance of thunderstorms possibly late Sunday afternoon.

Katrina was up early and fixed a hot cup of tea as she heard the boys get up to get ready for school. She poured grape juice into the small glasses for each child and set them on the table along with their favorite box of cereal, spoons, and bowls. Wayne was the first one to the table.

"Good morning Mom, are you still planning to be away when we get home from school this afternoon?" as he poured his cereal into one of the bowls.

"Junior, hurry and come to get your breakfast so you don't miss the bus." She yelled up the stairs. She then went to check on Rosa to see if she was a wake to get her ready for school. Rosa was picking out a short outfit and shirt to wear to school.

"Sweetie your shirt really doesn't match why not wear this shirt with the pink flowers and some ankle socks today?" as she took it out of the dresser drawer. "Then I will put up your hair into pony tails with matching bands."

"Okay Mommy, can I have a peanut butter and grape jelly sandwich for breakfast? Because I really don't like the cereal and is my lunch box packed." At the same time, Rosa slipped her feet into the pair of tennis shoes.

"I guess and yes I made your lunch. Today I made you a cheese sandwich, but you have sliced carrot sticks, a juice box, and cookies." Katrina answered her.

Katrina went to check on the boys and Wayne was already grabbing his back pack and heading to the front door. "Wait for your brother and sister please." She walked back down the hall toward the kitchen and Junior was just finishing putting his dishes into the sink. She made Rosa her PBJ and placed it on the table. Rosa ate her sandwich in a hurried fashion and grabbed her wind breaker to catch up with her brothers.

"Hey guys wait for me, I am coming!" she yelled.

"Junior did you brush your teeth?" she knew the answer.

"Yes mom and I have everything in my backpack," He responded. All three children went out the door to head for the bus. Katrina watched as the school bus stopped and the children got on to ride to the school. Now she would have time to clean up the kitchen from breakfast by putting the dishes into the dishwasher to run later. Then she would walk the dog for about ten minutes and jump into a shower to get dressed before going over to Prue's. Unfortunately, if she did not time this right she would not have enough time to finish packing her personal things into the overnight bag let alone get it into the car. It was already 9:30 and she had just got out of the shower. She put out the skirt and blouse that she would wear to the bed and breakfast on the hanging door hook. Placed all her personal things in a big zip lock bag and put them into the zipper part of the overnight bag. She dressed in a pair of jogging pants along with a t-shirt and placed the overnight bag in the garage then went out the door. She checked to make sure it was locked and headed over to Prue's house. She rang the doorbell before Prue finally opened it and told her to come on in.

"I will only be a few minutes, I thought maybe we would have a glass of lemonade while we worked today," she stated to Katrina.

Katrina watched her friend go up the stairs and into the small kitchen. She looked at Prue's face it was a little pale this morning because of the prescription's the physician kept her on for her Vertigo condition.

"Are you alright Prue? I will finish this embroidered pillow case and then I will need to be home around noon so I can change into another outfit. Dean is able to work from home today so he can be there when the children get home from school."

"They had asked me what I wanted for Mother's Day this year and I told them I wanted some quiet time so Dean told me to book a bed and breakfast place for two nights. What will you be doing this year for Mother's Day?" She waited for Prue to respond.

"I am just staying home, take my medication, or maybe watch some television with the family and have a few beers." Prue looked over at Katrina.

"Is everything alright, Prue?" She could tell today that her friend looked distraught.

"I am sorry Katrina, I did not sleep well last night and I wish our family had some money so I could do something like that or get me something that I really want for myself."

Katrina finished the second pillowcase and placed a price tag on it before putting it away inside the tote. She knew that her friend envied her because they always had some extra money saved aside to do a weekend away or eventually a family vacation. Katrina did not understand some of the jealous tendencies she showed when it came to Cassandra or Rosa.

"Well, I will be home around five o'clock on Sunday do you want me to call you that night or the next morning?" Katrina finished picking up and went to put her shoes on.

"No that is alright Katrina I will talk with you on Monday sometime in the afternoon before the children get home from school," was all she said as she continued to work on the fall color afghan.

"Okay I will talk with you later then. You have a Happy Mother's Day and weekend." She replied as she went out the front door.

KATRINA UNLOCKED THE door and went straight to the master bedroom to change so she could get on the road. She was anxious to leave but it took at least two or three hours to get to her destination. She dressed carefully, put a little bit of make-up on and her wedding ring set. She gave Dean a kiss good-bye and then went to the garage. She put her overnight bag on the floor in front of the front passenger seat. The sun coming through the van windows seemed warm so she put the AC on low and was on her way for a quiet weekend. She was glad to have the break from the children and family for only a few days. She turned on the radio's adult soft rock music and headed to the small town by the mighty Mississippi River. Katrina arrived around dinner time for she had stopped at a diner to order something to eat before arriving at the bread and breakfast place to check-in. Her stomach had a fluttery feeling as she saw the town nestled in the rolling hills of the valley. She found a parking spot and grabbed her overnight bag. The bed and breakfast was inside a Victoria style home from the Civil War era before the inn keeper came in from a small parlor room with a guest book.

"Good evening, may I have your name? My husband and I run this bread and breakfast inn year around. My name is Nancy O'Learry and my husband's name is Aaron. We have operated the Inn for about seven years now and we have five suites. We have three up stairs only one has its own bathroom with shower and two downstairs that have garden whirlpool baths along with a gas fireplace. These rooms are usually for honeymoon guests. I will take you upstairs to your room for the weekend. If there is anything you need just call the front desk by pushing this number on the phone." Nancy said with a smile.

"Thank you for all the information and I am sure that I will be fine." Katrina replied as she began to follow Nancy up the stairs to the second floor. The stairs had a mahogany railing all the way up and in the hall way a small table wooden table with an antique wash basin was on it. Katrina was already impressed with the dated antiques throughout the Victorian house and when Nancy opened the door to the room she thought the room was just beautiful.

"Here is your key to the room and we serve breakfast at eight in a family table fashion. Dinner on Saturday night begins at 5:30 but we are less formal because if the weather is nice we have a barbeque out on the brick patio surround by our English garden." Nancy handed her the key and left her to unpack her belongings. The room had a maroon color figurine turn of the century wallpaper and on the biggest wall a large four posted bed with a quilt that matched the wallpaper. The first thing she wanted to do was to get some lounging clothes on then grab her book to read on the swing located on one of the side porches. She also wanted to check out the parlor to see if they had any brochures to see if there were events going on in town that she might be interested in seeing or going too.

FTER DINNER SHE would have a glass of red Cabinet then go to bed so that she could get an early start in the morning. She would have to set a small alarm clock to wake her up at 7:15 so that she would have enough time to get down to the breakfast. She struggled at first by toss but eventually fell asleep. The small alarm clock begun to beep for several minutes before Katrina was awake enough to roll over to turn it off and got up for the day's activities. She washed up; put her spring top on with a pair of khaki shorts and tennis shoes. After breakfast she would worry about putting on some make-up and jewelry. She made it to breakfast with the other people that were staying at the inn. Nancy had eight table settings on a long table in a formal dining room with many antique pieces including a beautiful Victorian style hutch that had grape, apple, and orange juice in pitchers for people to pour for themselves. Nancy had particularly spend much of time with preparing the kish, apple turnovers, tarts, muffins and an egg casserole for everyone to serve themselves. I took a little of each of the foods before asking to be excused.

"The breakfast was filling and delightful, Nancy. What time will dinner be served? I am going to walk into town later this morning to visit the small antique shops, niches, and specialty stores. I should be back sometime around three this afternoon. I contacted one of the ladies that usually come out to the bed & breakfast inns to give massages and I have a scheduled appointment for four o'clock."

"We will have dinner for everyone around 5:30 tonight, as a rule, so that our guest can unwind after their day." Nancy replied with a smile, "Have a nice day, if there is anyone interested I do have more brochures in the den that are updated from the town arts center."

"I would like one please, especially, if there are in local festivals or wine tastings going on this weekend." Katrina said as she patiently waited for Nancy to return with the brochures' before going back to her room to finish getting ready to go on her day's adventure. She began to read the brochure and walk up the stairs. She unlocked the room and took out her make-up bag from the zipper side of the overnight bag. She sat on the bed and put her make-up on, she lightly but the base on then blended it in, next she added a light green eye shadow on her eyes along with mascara since she wore glasses to make her eyes stand out just little. She put a pair of ear-rings in and a bangle bracelet. Especially, now she was ready to go into town for a while and if nothing else to do some window shopping. Nearly, took her 20 minutes to come to the first shop which was busy with workers making fresh homemade fudge. She took a sample of the chocolate raspberry swirl and then decided only to get a half pound of the maple fudge which was one of her favorites. The next stop was filled with designer scarves, purses of all sizes or colors of spring, and costume jewelry. She picked out a pair of bangle bracelets along with matching earrings' as a gift for her mom since her birthday was only a few weeks away. The next shop on Main Street was an antique shop and she browsed for several minutes then stopped at the corner Bistro for a croissant ham sandwich for lunch. She decided since it was a nice spring day that she would eat it outside at one of the patio tables. She sat eating her sandwich with a cold glass of lemonade and looked over the small brochure map. She watched the other people walk up and down the street going into the stores. She finished her lunch and began to walk to the specialty store and her last stop would be at the winery store. She would cross the street at the next light and stop at a garden and lace shop. She bought a few garden knick knacks and headed to the winery. The winery store had wine tasting with crackers and cheese to serve to their customers; along with wine that was local, wine glasses of all style, and wine saying t-shirts. Although it was time to head back she noticed that she would stop at the next shop which was a gallery if only for a few minutes to looked at the handcrafted pottery and art work of local artist.

She made it back in plenty of time for the massage and then it would be time for dinner. After dinner she would go back to the side porch and read on the swing. The time seemed to go by quickly and it was starting to get dark. She laid out her clothes for the morning and put all her packages at the bottom of her overnight bag. She was relaxed and turned in early for bed. She would check out at noon and stop on the way home at a historical mark and museum. The weekend had gone quickly and was saddened by it, but now she could come back in the future with Dean. The next morning she got up almost too late for breakfast and when she got to the table the other guest had already ate and had checked-out. Katrina was glad because she really wasn't in the mood for conversation. Nancy walked into the parlor to pick up the remaining dished.

"Did I miss breakfast this morning? I guess I was tired more than I thought."

"Almost, I'll just leave this tray out and if there is anything else I can get you this morning, "she asked.

"No I only wanted a piece of toast with honey, a cup of hot tea, and a glass of orange juice. Thank you anyway," Katrina replied.

"I hope your visit was a relaxing one and you will come back soon to visit us," Nancy then walked out the room. She went back to the room to get her belongings and take them to the van. She went back inside the Victorian house to pay the bill and leave the key. There was an entry way table with a basket and a vase filled with fresh cut tulips. The basket was for guest to put their room key in and then she located Nancy in another area of the house.

"I would like to pay my bill. I hope that in the future my husband and I can come here to stay for a weekend get-a-way."

"Well you can sign our guest book and write down your email address," Nancy replied.

"I have already done that but thank you," said Katrina.

Once she paid the bill she started her trip home. She turned on a radio station the announcer had just put out a severe weather alert to all the counties. Katrina drove home and as she turned into her drive way it started to rain.

When she opened the door she could hear the children along with Dean in the kitchen.

"Hi everyone." She stated. When she entered the kitchen and dining area; she noticed the table had a yellow tablecloth on and a dozen of red roses as a center piece. The table had been set and Dean was just about done preparing the meal.

"Honey, why don't you go put your overnight bag in our bedroom and come back to eat dinner," as he pulled a spiral ham out of the oven.

"Mom we all took turns helping Dad today so we could surprise you with a special dinner," Said Wayne.

"Mommy, I helped in setting the table," Rosa was showing her the job she had done.

"Well, everything looks lovely and I'm ready to eat," she replied. She left the room and put the overnight bag on the floor in the bedroom then came back and sat in her chair at the table. The meal was excellent and everything made her weekend a memorable one.

Rosa's birthday party with her girl friends from school seemed to pass by quickly by along with Mother's Day and the craft fair at the end of the month of May.

The days seemed to get longer along with the warmer temperatures quickly the weeks of June had arrived and all the children were out of school for summer break. The public swimming pool once again was open from nine in the morning for those individual's that may want their children into swim lessons then; at one in the afternoon it was opened for open swim to everyone that had a amenities pool pass. Dean and the boys would be gone for a week at summer camp. Katrina and Rosa were looking forward on leaving for a week by flying to Buffalo, New York. They were going to a family reunion and she was going to rent a car so she could take Rosa to see attractions or museums in the area. She had already made her reservations at the hotel and reserved the sedan for the week. They would arrive in Buffalo the Thursday before the family reunion which this year would be around the 19th of July. She was anxious about seeing cousins, aunts, friends of the family, and a chance to show Rosa where she grew up at, especially the family cabin near Watertown, New York. She was going to meet her parents' there since they left in their motor home weeks ago from the four corners area. They were already on the east coast visiting family and friends.

The last weekend in June their little community would celebrate the Fourth of July festivities. Starting Friday evening, there would be a pie eating contest, a baseball tournament and a sand volleyball tournament

Then Saturday morning a horseshoe tournament, a decorative bike contest and a parade with a float contest. Starting around five o'clock, brats, corn-on-the-cob, and other concessions of food were available for families to have a picnic. At dusk the local patrols would close off a street for dancing with a D.J.; along with local bands played in the grass and the last would be a night filled with colorful fireworks presentation. Sunday morning there would be a denomination church program held outside in a tent if the weather was nice. Katrina had coordinated with Bobby Joe and Douglas Skinner to meet their families by the outside of the public basketball courts near the lake to watch the fireworks.

Dean was taking some more of his vacation time by taking off that Friday and Monday.

"Junior, can you please go into the garage and see if the blanket we use to set on is there?" She had already put the folding chairs in the family van. In getting ready for the weekend events.

Junior quickly went out into the garage.

"Mom the big color squared blanket is here and I put it on the van seat. Is that all I need to do?"

She would not pack the cooler or picnic basket until the morning. Dean would need to stop on the way home after work to pick up odds and ends for the busy weekend. She started to write a check list down so things would not be forgotten

"Okay, we have the blanket and folding chairs in the van. We will need mosquito spray, sun block, the first aid kit, sand toys, Frisbee, towels, a change of clothes for Junior and Rosa, paper towels or/and moist towelettes just in case someone really gets dirty. Is there anything else that I am missing on this list?" Katrina would leave the list on the refrigerator with a magnet just in case other items would need to be added in the future. She still had eight days left before the weekend and that was plenty of time for things to get done. Since, Prue's conversation was still bothering her about the seriousness of the topic. The conversation with Prue most of the time was about their husbands, children, the teachers or education, crafts, and planting a garden Katrina didn't expect that the upcoming months would soon more than just a learning experience about the court system, yet emotional escapade. She would learn that Prue was a manipulator when it came to the justice system which would allow people to see who she really was. She would lose much more than anyone could imagine once it was all over and her life would be turned upside down. However, Prue had contacted the states attorney's office to file a complaint against her and was irreconcilable when they saw one another out in public areas.

It was after lunch and some of Wayne's friends had ridden their bikes to their house. They were in the family room playing a new game on the computer. A few of Junior's classmates had also dropped by to play on the computer before going to the little league game.

"Yes, Wayne now you can go back and play with your friends' on the computer,' she said. Cassandra had stopped by on her bike to pick up Rose so that they could ride their bikes down to the public pool. She was glad that Rose was now old enough to go by herself.

"Rose don't forget a beach towel and sun block. Did you get the bike lock off the rack?" She was busy cleaning the kitchen up from everyone having a snack.

"Mom what time do I need to be home?" Rose replied as she went toward the garage to leave.

The door bell rang and she didn't know who it might be since it was so close to dinner time. She went to answer the door.

"Good evening, I have a subpoena for you Mrs. Katrina Garrett; my name is Detective Malone." He held a piece of paper up that looked like an official document and handed it to her to read.

"What are you talking about detective," was all she could say.

Detective Malone waited for her to finish reading the document.

"You will be contacted by the Department of Child and Family Services to be investigated for neglect and you will need to appear on the given court date." Was all Detective Malone could say and then he went back to his car and left.

"What was the detective talking about?" she was about to cry; as the detective was in an unmark car. Shortly afterwards, Rose rode up with her bike back into the garage to park it. Cassandra didn't stay long afterwards because she needed to get home for dinner.

"Rose get back in the house! I need to immediately call your dad. Plus, right now I don't want you to play or associate with Cassandra anymore." She stated.

"Mom what did I do wrong this time?" Rose was beginning to whimper and did not understand.

"You did not do anything Rose" then the tears began to go down her pink cheeks.

"Mom what is it?" Junior said in a more serious tone of voice as he approached the living room.

She went to the phone and dialed Dean's cell number.

"Dean, I am scared. A county detective came by this evening to hand me a subpoena for neglect and I'm being sued for it. The detective would or could not tell me who filed such an outrageous allegation." She was still upset about the detective's strange visit as she talked with Dean.

"The detective that came to the house was medium built, black curly hair and wore a suit and tie.

"I have never seen him in the area before and his name does not ring any bells. Do you think that your friend that is a retired fire chief knows him or a good attorney to take such a case?" She stated.

"Let me make a few phone calls and I will call you back Katrina," Dean replied.

"Katrina, just try to keep it together and I am sure that it is just a misunderstanding," Dean wanted to assure Katrina that everything would be okay yet she was beside herself. She had told Wayne and Junior's friends that they would need to leave and go back home.

Dean made his phone calls and called in some favors from his friends before heading home. However, she was a basket case when Dean finally came home for the night. They were really wandering who contacted the states attorney office and pressed such allegations against her. She had never been arrested, she only had one ticked for speeding and that was over five years ago. She needed to call Bobby Jo about having Wayne, Junior and Rose over the next morning while they went to the county court house early to meet with the attorney Dean had called on the way home from his work cell phone. Dean had found a local attorney by the name of Jack Steward from the law offices of Steward, Livingston and Parish. He would be meeting them at 8:30 A.M. in a second floor room at the county courthouse. It was after ten o'clock when she called Bobby Jo and she was hoping she had not gone to bed for the night.

The phone was on its third ring and Bobby Jo's voice was on the phone.

"Bobby Jo did I wake you?" She hesitated for a moment.

"No Katrina, I was just watching a movie and had dozed off. What do you need?" Bobby Jo was groggy but Katrina had her attention.

"I hate to ask this, but I need you to watch the children early tomorrow probably until five o'clock? Dean and I need to be at the courthouse by nine. After we get back from court; then I can explain what the heck is going on and get answers for all of us.

"Sure Katrina that won't be a problem. Just make sure that each of them has an extra set of clothes in case they play outside in the sandbox. I will see you tomorrow and everything will be okay. Bye."

"See you in the morning, bye." She hung up the phone. She knew that Bobby Jo was trying to be positive but Katrina just did not know what to make of the subpoena and the allegations it was making about her.

The boys were playing a game on the entertainment center and Rose was watching her brothers play. Every now and then she would get up and go over to her toy box and get a Barbie out with a new outfit to put on it.

"Mom can you help me put this dress on this Barbie, please." Rosa handed the doll and dress to her.

"I will put the dress on but you will need to get dressed for bed and I will be in there in a few minutes." She answered her. Rosa went to her room to get ready for bed. She followed her daughter into the bedroom with the Barbie.

"Are you going to sleep with your Barbie tonight?" She tucked Rosa under the covers.

"I have a surprise for you; tomorrow morning Dad and I are dropping you off to play with Danaka all day.

"Are Junior and Wayne going with me to their house?"

"Yes, they are because Dad and I have to be in Belvidere for an appointment with an attorney." She did not want to upset the children by telling them why they were really going at least not yet until they had some more information. Then she would tell them individually when the time was right. She sat on the side of the bed as Rosa drifted off to sleep. Wayne and Junior had already gone to bed. She went to check on each of them. She knew tonight she would have problems sleeping because of the next day. She saw Dean in bed but he had left the television on again. She turned it off and climbed into bed. She was exhausted but for the next hour or so she tossed and turned in bed. She finally drifted off to sleep but was woken up by the alarm clock. She slowly got up and jumped into the shower. She had laid out a conservative pants suit out to wear to court. When she got out of the shower Dean was no longer in the bedroom, she could hear commotion in the kitchen along with Wayne and Rose's voices. Dean had gotten up with them to give them breakfast while she took her time to get ready. She was dressed in a navy pants suit with a white blouse, and very little make-up. She walked into the kitchen to see her children eating pancakes and sausage. Dean was in front of the stove and putting batter into the skillet to make another yummy pancake.

"Good morning Wayne and Rosa. Good morning honey, the pancakes smell delicious." She gave Dean a kiss on the cheek.

Rosa's mouth was full of pancake as she tried to talk. "Mommy, Wayne said that he is not going to play over at Danaka's house today." Syrup was dripping from the corner of her mouth.

"Mom what is Rosa talking about?' he asked as he put his juice glass down.

"I will talk to all of you at once when Junior comes in here for breakfast." Junior walks into the kitchen with his shirt inside out to sit down for breakfast.

"Mom can I have a glass of chocolate milk with my breakfast?" Junior took a bite of his toast.

"I guess you can have some chocolate milk as long as you eat all of your breakfast. I also need you to fix your shirt that is inside out." She looked over to Wayne snickering at his brother.

"Wayne finishes your breakfast then help in getting your sister ready to leave. Rose was right about the play day with Danaka, Patrick and Randall. Dad and I have an important meeting to go to this morning and will be back this evening.

"Mom is about the man that stopped here yesterday to see you?" Junior looked at Wayne and then at her. She could see that he was confused.

"Yes, kind of and I will tell you more later when Dad and I come tonight to pick you up."

"Okay Mom I think I understand," as he got up from the table and put his dirty glass into the sink. Then he went to look for Wayne and get his flip flops to put on before getting into the van.

They all got into the van and left for Bobby Jo's house. She looked at her watch and they were running late as usual maybe the attorney would not be waiting for them.

Dean pulled up into the drive way and put it into park.

"I will take the kids in along with the back pack and I should not be very long. I know we need to get going because of the time." she opened the door and got out to open the sliding door of the van.

Wayne had already unbuckled and was helping Junior get his bag from under the seat.

Rose was out first and began to run toward the door. Then Wayne and Junior followed with Katrina coming behind them. The door was already being opened by Danaka and Rose had slipped off her sandals to follow her up the bi-level stair case. Junior and Wayne went downstairs to the playroom to find Patrick.

"Katrina, are you alright?" Bobby Jo was in the kitchen picking up from breakfast.

"I am fine but I cannot stay, here are the extra clothes and a box of macaroni and cheese for lunch. Do you want me to shut the front door behind me?" she waited for a quick reply.

"No go ahead and leave it open for now, there is a nice summer breeze going through the house."

"Thanks for everything you are a life saver," Katrina yelled as she went out the door. Now she got back into the van and put her seatbelt on. She still felt nauseated and could hardly eat this morning because of a nervous stomach. She had never been in trouble with the law let alone inside a courtroom. She wasn't sure what to expect and Dean had not said a word on the drive into town.

"Dean are you sure that this attorney will be able to help and take my case?" She looked over to see if he would respond. He did not answer as he parked the van. She had butterflies in her stomach from being nervous, anxious and scared.

The attorney was waiting in front of the doors of the courthouse. Attorney Jack Steward was short and stocky in built even in his tailored suit and maroon colored tie. He was partial bald with a salt and pepper mustache well groomed. He had a gruff voice when he spoke to his clients.

"Good morning Mr. and Mrs. Garrett, I am Attorney Jack Steward and I have looked over the allegations that the States Attorney has gathered so far against you as a neglected parent. I have reserved a room on the second floor near courtroom A. Do you have any questions at this time?" He put a leather briefcase, emptied his pockets into a container, and put his jacket into another basket to go through the security scan. She only had a small hand purse that had to be checked through the scan and then she walked through a full body scan. Dean had to follow suit and met up with them at the stairs.

"We only have about twenty minutes before going into the courtroom before Judge MacGuire. Is there anything you can tell me that is not on the subpoena about the charges?" He looked at her for a response.

"I am sorry Mr. Steward, but I am not sure what this is all about. Maybe if you can give more information about the charges that were given to the States Attorney or police department. I can give you answers." She wasn't sure what he wanted from her at this time.

"Do you know that you are being sued for $135,000 for neglect, child endangerment, and medical? The person who is suing you is for damages to her daughter Cassandra while she was at your house sometime around Mother's Day. There will be a deposition in a few weeks for you, Dean, Rose and Wayne to be done for the courts." Attorney Jack Steward now explained more and now she understood why Prue had asked so many questions in the past few months.

"If you need to use the bathroom or a drink from the water fountain you should do it now before going into the courtroom." Attorney Jack Steward began to put the file in his attaché case and they left the room together.

"I am going to the ladies room, I feel a little light headed from today's events and I will meet you inside the courtroom." She stated to Dean and now her attorney. She went into the ladies room only to find a roll of paper towels where she took a few sheets and moistened them with cool water. She rub her forehead and back of her neck. She had not been able to eat since the detective came by the house. She took a few deep and slow breaths then walked toward the courtroom. She opened the big wooden door and found Dean sitting on the right side in one of the hard wooden benches. She was thankful that the Judge had not entered the courtroom.

She was just about to sit down when a man next to a side entrance stood up to state that the court was now in session. The man was from African American descendent and reached over six feet in height. He had a stern face when he introduced the judge and he was serious about his duties inside the courtroom. Attorney Jack Steward was sitting on her right and leaned over to whisper in her ear the name of the bail lift.

"His name is Dominick McFadden; he has been the bail left officer for at least ten years," Jack whispered.

"Please rise for Judge Jeremiah MacGuire, his court is now in session." The officer stated.

Everyone in the courtroom stood up and Judge MacGuire took the bench.

"You may be seated, the number on the docket states this is a civil suit but may also be more. Has the state attorney contacted the Department of Children and Family Services for questioning the children involved?" He asked the attorney's in the courtroom.

They both replied, "Yes your honor."

"I have also requested that the daughter of the Garrett's, Rose to be taken to the Lynn Donald's Center for abuse to be interviewed along with other girls that have been at their house," States Attorney Morgana Delta-Serpentine.

Katrina watched the courtroom like it was a nightmare unfolding. The States Attorney Morgana Delta-Serpentine kept looking over at her and discussing the neglect charges against her because she was a stay at home mom. Katrina noticed this tall but slender woman was dressed in a conservative gray pin-striped suit, little makeup and her blond hair was styled and shoulder length. The women matched her name of Serpentine according to the town's newspaper. She was hard core for neglected parents, abuse, and sex offenders which meant she had a high success of putting these individual's in jail for more than a year. She used any means to get the verdict of guilty charged hence the way she collected evidence was usually sneaky and slithered just above the fine line of the law. Now she understand how the nickname of the States Attorney Serpentine or known in the community as Cobra.

"I have will be taking the children so they can be questioned. Her mother is the person that filed the report at our office because Cassandra is a minor," Cobra stated to the court recorder that was sitting by the bench. The middle age woman was transcribing everything that was being said inside the court room. The woman was dressed in khaki pants with a sweater because the courtroom was quite chilly.

The court room had several benches in a row; there were five on the left side and an aisle in the center to walk and another five on the right all made with the same type of dark wood. Along the left wall a few seats enough to hold a jury in necessary and another chair where a police officer or security officer would seat. Next was a railing and in front two tables on either side with several chairs for the attorney's and the defendant. The large podium was solid wood with Judge MacGuire wearing a black robe. The gavel, official documents and a pitcher of water with a glass was in front of him. Right next to him was a small table with the Bible on it and a witness chair with a microphone for the person to talk into it about the truth. Katrina was wandering now if the court really knew what the truth really was or was a person guilty automatically and had to be found innocent.

Dean had called in some favors and hired a top notch lawyer that dealt with juvenile cases. She was waiting outside the courtroom to talk to them and tell them about what the charges were against Wayne. It looked like they would be in court all day with only an hour for lunch. Katrina knew that with the way she was feeling there was no way she would be able to eat because her stomach felt like someone had just hit her and she would not be able to keep anything down.

"Mrs. Garrett do you understand these charges and in the next week the court will ask individual's to come in for a deposition. Attorney Steward, do you have any questions at this time?" Judge MacGuire stated in a stern voice.

"Does your client understand everything that was said today?" States Attorney Cobra said in a high pitch tone to make a point.

"Yes your Honor my client Mrs. Garrett understands," Attorney Steward stated.

"We will meet back here in two weeks to see if there is any new evidence. What day will that be Ms. Moon?" Judge MacGuire looked out to wait for everyone to look at their schedules.

"Mr. Steward and Ms. Delta-Serpentine will this date work for you? It is October 6, a Tuesday at nine o'clock in court room two." Judge MacGuire had Ms. Moon schedule it. "Court is now adjourning," as he hit the gavel on the table and then got up from his chair.

"Will everyone please rise," the bail lift announced as the judge exited the courtroom.

The bail lift then walked to the big heavy doors to open them for the next case on the docket. She was confused about the of the law jargon and she was sure that some of the stuff that had been said between Prue and her in the past was going to be brought in front of the court but she was not sure of exactly what at this time. Now everyone in her family was not allowed to contact Prue or Cassandra to find out what went on that given day that the court was now questioning Katrina about and her calendar. The woman sitting at a round table engrossed in reading over a file in another small conference room next to the court house law library.

The attorney that was waiting was from the Attorney's Weatherspoon, Carpenter, & Smithson, LLC that we had hired for their son's juvenile case. The young woman was dressed professionally in a navy skirt suit, a cotton beige blouse and pumps. She had strawberry blonde hair that was in a pixie style. She seemed homely to Katrina yet, very knowledgeable with the state juvenile laws.

"Good afternoon Mr. and Mrs. Garrett, my name is Jammie Weatherspoon I will be the advocate in the juvenile case.

She listened to Ms. Weatherspoon explain why it was a necessity for her to be there. Dean was asking questions and discussed the alternatives. She was physically there but not mentally she felt like she was in a nightmare that she could not wake up from. She wanted to go home have a few shots of Rum, take a shower and go to bed. She went to bed but really did not sleep except when she did drink; this would soon stop when her parent's arrived then around them she would need to hide her true self. Ms. Weatherspoon was gathering her papers and putting them in her briefcase.

"Katrina, Mrs. Garrett do you have any questions for me?" Ms. Weatherspoon was looking at her waiting.

She looked at in a blank stare. "No Ms.Weatherspoon I currently cannot think of any right now, but thank you any ways."

"Sweetheart, we should get going." Dean was in a hurry to get home.

Katrina did not know why he was being so impatient. The home they all knew for the last ten years was being torn apart by each strain of fiber. Judge MacGuire motion to have the depositions done in a month only made things drag on forever.

THEY LEFT THE court house around 4:30 today; she knew she should be famished since all she had for breakfast this morning was a hot cup of tea and a piece of buttered toast. Unfortunately nothing look good today or most days except for a blue martini at times a marguerite. She focused on her community college classes in business when she was around people but when she was alone all she wanted to do was drink alcohol until it made her sleepy. Then she would sleep without dreaming.

Dean drove home and she looked out the van window watching the scenery pass by like a fast forward on a DVD player. She noticed they were already home and pulling into the garage. Wayne would be going to Bobby Jo's house tomorrow after we picked up Junior and Rosa in the morning. We would also have to pick up Danaka since she was staying with us a temporary solution for the courts. Once her parent's would arrive then she had to ask them to take custody of the children. She did not want the state to get a hold of them even though the Cobra wanted to lock up Wayne and throw away the key. Bobby Jo had received the documentation that their family had to follow why Wayne was staying there. The deposition for herself was scheduled in three weeks. The court wanted a psychological profile done on Wayne and Rosa. Dean's deposition was scheduled for next week. She was losing her whit and second guessing everything.

"Dean do you think I am a good mom to our children?" she looked at him with misty eyes.

"Honey you do a lot with our children and yes you are a good mom and wife," he replied. "Why do you ask such silly questions? I love you and you did not do anything wrong." Dean looked at his wife and gave her a hug.

She did not feel relieved at all and inside she just wanted to scream at the world.

She looked at her messages and noticed that her mom had called and left a message she listened to it.

"Katrina it is your Mom, we are parked at the Lazy J Campground right outside of town. We want to know what is going on since you would not tell us over the phone a few days ago. Dad and I are worried. Please call or come out to the campground." She hung up the phone.

Katrina would have to explain everything to them in person.

"Dean Do you think you can watch Rosa, Danaka, and Junior this evening? My parent's arrived sometime today while we were in court. I need to discuss with them if they will take guardianship."

Dean looked at his wife, "I don't see why not. Do you really want to do this by yourself?"

She hesitated, "Yes it is the only way, since the neglected charges are against me not you."

The last few days had been long and tiresome for her. She walked through the door and headed to the bedroom to change her clothes. She wanted to put some shorts and a t-shirt on before going to the campground. She first needed a shot of tequila before doing anything. She had stashed a fifth in the corner of her closet. While she was getting her clothes she reached for the bottle and then took two gulps. Then she changed quickly as she heard Dean heading toward her. She placed the bottle in the corner for another time like tomorrow morning she would want another quick drink or maybe she would have an Irish coffee.

"Is everything alright Katrina?" he had to check on her she was taking longer than normal to change and get going. He was worried about her she was keeping to herself more and always had her nose in the college book.

She had stashed the bottle just in time. She slipped on her t-shirt and went into the bathroom to quickly brush her teeth.

"I am just about ready, just finished getting ready," as she walked out and grabbed her purse.

"I will see you in a little bit." and gave him a kiss good bye. She got into the driver's side of the van and opened the garage door. The girls were in

Rosa's room playing and Junior had been downstairs since they had gotten home. He was being quieter than normal and began playing one of the video games for the Playstation. He was in his own world since the day the sheriff had stopped by a few weeks ago. She had made an appointment with Dr. McDoodle for Junior. The court's had another psychiatrist that worked with cases for Rosa and Wayne.

She was taking the back road to the Lazy J before she knew it she was there and pulled into the office to register as a guest. She went into the office and an older woman was behind the counter.

"Good afternoon welcome to Lazy J Campgrounds. Can I help you? Hi my name is Dotty."

"Yes thank you I am a guest visiting my parents here at the campground, there name is Peabody. I believe they are staying here for a couple of weeks." Katrina was anxious but at the same time nervous about seeing her mom and dad. Her dad had retired last fall so they could travel but now they would have to give that up because of her predicament.

"Let me see now, you did say Peabody right?" she was flipping through registration papers. Oh yes here they are Mr. & Mrs. Floyd Peabody. They are at site 25 because they are in a self contained RV. Here is a pass to put inside your vehicle, just lay it on the dash so the person that checks can see that you are a guest and registered here at the office."

"Thank you Dotty, she filled out the form and handed it back to her. Dotty handed her a pass."

"Just make sure before you leave for the evening that you place the pass in the side slot there. Since tomorrow the pass is a different color. Of course if you decide that you are staying the night then I would give you this color pass and charge you five dollars. Your parents have already paid me for two weeks."

Katrina opened the office door and a warm humid breeze hit her face. She climbed back into the driver's side of the van and rolled down the window. She slowly drove on the gravel road and looking for the numbers posted on wooden stakes. She made a left turn and she could see her parent's RV underneath some trees. They were able to get a shady site. She parked the van behind the RV and took some deep breaths. She was going to leave the window down just a little and then closed the door.

She went around the corner and saw her parent's sitting at a picnic table playing a game of cards. They had not seen her pull in.

"Hi mom and dad, how was the drive in?"

Ruthann looked at her daughter and waited to see if the grandkids would run up to say hi any minute.

"Where is everyone else did Rosa and Junior come with you?"

"Mom the kids stayed with Dean this time, I will bring them out to see you tomorrow. I needed to talk to you and dad first. Dean thought it was best that the kids stayed with him so we would not be distracted."

"Mom I can show you some photos in just a minute, but first I have some disturbing news about what has happened," she looked at Floyd and Ruthanne.

Her mom stood up and gave her a hug. She went to her dad and gave him a kiss on the cheek.

"Hi kiddo what was going on that you couldn't tell us over the phone." He sat down his hand of cards.

"It cannot be that bad is it?" He looked at his daughter and her eyes were tearing up.

"Mom and dad sit down. I will tell you everything and then the question I will eventually ask. I want you both to think about it over night before giving Dean and me an answer."

"I am not even sure where to begin. I guess I will start from the day right before the Fourth of July. I am only going to summarize everything because I still don't understand everything that is going on." She took a deep breath and continued to tell them about the evening when the sheriff had came to the house. She had her parents' attention and they listened to her tell them what happened.

The sheriff had brought a subpoena for me and told me I had to be in small claims court. They were also there to take Wayne in custody for allegations that a person had filed at the States Attorney's office. The sheriff did not hand me any paperwork they just put him in the squad car. We have been going to the courthouse a couple a days a week to meet with attorneys and in the courtroom in front of a judge.

Ruthanne looked at Katrina, "Do you think he did anything?"

"I don't know if he did or not apparently he was babysitting on the day being questioned and Dean was on his way home from work but was running late as usual." "The attorney said I was a neglected mother because I was not home that night and I did not know what my children were doing 24/7." "The deposition for me is next week but I am sure that the judge will want to meet you since the family is being picked apart. However, according to them I only have two children because the sheriff department left something at the house. He gave it to Junior while we were in court. Junior cannot be questioned because he read the file and the attorney's said that any information from him was now tainted."

"So what were the charges, exactly?" Floyd asked his daughter.

"Dad on July 8th Judge MacGuire made a notice of Serving Discovery. Then I have to go to the court house on July 26th to answer the plaintiff's complaint at Law Proof of Service. The next court date for a hearing will be sometime in August. I know that the Honorable MacGuire will want to meet with you on the behalf of Wayne and possibly Junior. Unfortunately, there are particulars that I have some of the paperwork for, but we will introduce the attorneys that are covering the case so you can ask any questions or might have concerns about."

"The Children and Family Services are trying to sort out everything and wonder if there is any sexual abuse that happened. I am the one currently under investigation and the courts are waiting to press additional charges.

Ruthanne shook her head and did not say a word.

"Mom and Dad now do you understand why I could not talk about it over the phone. Now this is a hard part for me to do, Dean and I need to know if you can take Wayne's guardianship? Since, I am under investigation by the judge along with department of child and family services have taken all my parental rights. I know dad that you just started retirement but we don't want our son to be lost in the system or foster care. I would not ask this of you both but I have no other alternative. Would you be willing to become his guardianship and have him live with you in case he doesn't return home?"

"I want you to think about the answer because you have already raised your children. Think about it and discuss it tonight."

Floyd looked at his daughter, "Your mother and I don't need to discuss it if we need to take him in or to appointments we are here for all of you. I think your mother will agree that it is better for him to be with family."

"Mom and dad I don't want you to regret it for four or more years in the future," She stated.

"Enough bad news for now, the sun is setting and in the morning I am going to tell the kids that you are here so I am sure that they will want to come out to the campground to see you," she grabbed her purse to get the photos she kept with her.

"Mom here are the new photos I have of the children. This is one of Rosa winning the first place trophy in figure skating. The one of Junior and Wayne are from the little league team they are playing on this year. This one is of Wayne at the bowling alley," she handed each photo to her mom and then passed to her dad.

"Boy Katrina Wayne and Junior have grown from the last time we saw them. Rosa looks like a sweet young lady," her mom was wondering exactly when the last time she had seen her grandchildren.

"Katrina when was the last time we saw the children?" her dad could not believe how tall the children had grown.

"The last time was probably during the family reunion that was held in July 2001 in Norfolk, Virginia. Then Dean and the boys were taking their vacation together while Rosa and I went to the reunions. Then we started taking separate vacations every year since." Katrina responded to her parents.

"I think you are right, boy it has been over a year since we have seen Junior and Wayne," Ruthanne couldn't believe that Wayne was now taller than her.

Rosa will probably want to stay overnight if that is okay with you," Katrina gave her mom and dad both hugs before saying good bye. We will see around lunch time tomorrow." Then she climbed into the driver's side and started the van.

All the way home she cried about everything she was an emotional mess but was happy that her parent's understood the situation. She would need to ask again if they would regret taking in Wayne.

The next morning Katrina watched the sunrise over the lake and sipped her hot tea. She liked it when no one else had gotten up and she could think about the turn of events. She heard some noise in the upstairs bathroom. It was Rosa and she was up.

"Mommy what are we doing today?"

Katrina smiled and said, "I have a surprise for you and Junior so you will need to eat breakfast and get dressed for the day. Then we will be able to leave and you might want to take an extra pair of clothes in your little back pack."

"Where are we going?" Rosa sat at the kitchen table.

"Can I have some bacon this morning with chocolate milk?"

"I guess and she began frying up the bacon, the smell went through the house." She made four slices before Junior came into the room already dressed in his play clothes. Well I am glad that you are dressed I will take you to a place that is a surprise so I need you to eat and then brush your teeth. Junior before we go pack another outfit in a back pack just in case."

"Mom, where are we going? Are we going to go see Wayne?" he looked at her waiting for a reply.

"I know you miss your brother but one day you will see him. No the surprise is something different so you will need to wait." She was not smiling anymore it sadden her heart that the two boys could not see one another.

"Why can't I see him mom?" he asked

"The courts say that you and Rosa cannot see him right now, but maybe once we start counseling then you can see him." This was the only answer she had for him now and deep down she was hoping that things would change and Wayne would come home. Days went by the court days changed several times because the defense did not what they needed from everyone.

Rosa and Junior finished up eating and was getting ready. She washed out the dishes and left them in the sink. She went and put some cut offs on and a blue tank. It was going to be another hot humid day and she wanted to be comfortable. She buckled Rose's booster seat then helped Junior with the seat belt. They were on their way to a surprise. Junior kept asking what the surprise was and trying to guess.

"Is it an ice cream place? To a park? To an indoor play area?" He was going to keep asking her until she would get irritated enough to tell him. Except this time it was not going to work. She drove southeast out of town onto some back roads. She saw the sign for Lazy J Campground and turned down the gravel road.

Junior and Rosa were looking out the van windows. They came to a small building where she parked the van but left it running with the air conditioner going.

"Okay I have to run in here to register and get our pass then we will almost be there are you guys ready for the surprise?"

"Mom where are we really a campground, we did not bring any camping gear with us." He stated and stared back out the window.

Katrina shut the van door quickly to keep as much of the cooler air inside. She opened the door to the small office and grocery mart. The air conditioner was on too and it felt really nice. She went to the counter to sign in and get the guest pass. She wandered what child would want to stay the night. Then she noticed next to the cash register a small bookcase with novels for adults, some children books, a small collection of DVD's and VHS to rent or trade. She glanced at the collection of movies. She found a Disney VHS movie she thought the children would enjoy and rented it. It was only a couple of dollars for the weekend then it had to be back by Monday night at six.

"Excuse me is this all the Disney VHS movies you have here? Hi Dotty how you this morning?"

"Good morning, welcome to Lazy J. It looks like it's going to be another hot day. Yes that is all the DVD's we have there might be more tonight when people turn them in," she replied.

"I will just take this one for today, thanks Dotty. How much is the VHS?"

"Only a $1.75 and return back in two days," Dotty took the $2.00 from Katrina and rang up the sale.

"Keep the change or put it in the cup for the next person that might be short with cash," she statement.

Katrina signed the guest list then took the pass and VHS to the van. She got into the driver's seat of the van.

"Mom what took so long," Junior was beginning to fidget.

"I was just talking to the woman in the store and I got a VHS for you both to watch,"

"Watch where?" Rosa chimed in.

"You will see I need you to look for a number 25 on the post just like that one." She was driving caution so she could see the numbers."

"Mom we are at number 20." Rosa was looking too.

She could see the back of the RV

"Okay guys we are here!" she parked and turned off the van.

Junior was unbuckled and had the door opened and took off to see what mom was talking about.

Katrina unbuckled Rosa and helped her out of the van. She ran after her brother. Katrina grabbed the pack backs and shut the door.

"Hi Nana and Papa," she gave them a hug. Junior was already sitting by Papa in a folding chair.

"Mom when did Nana and Papa get here?" Rosa was looking at her. She was sitting at the picnic table next to Nana.

"They drove into Illinois yesterday and will be here for a couple of weeks. Mom I rented one of the VHS movies from the camp office for the kids to watch here this afternoon."

"I think Dad is taking Junior this afternoon fishing. Do you have a couple of dollars to buy some bait?" She handed Katrina a flyer that the campground had given them when they registered.

"Well I have five dollars on me but before they go fishing I want to discuss what I asked yesterday with the both of you. The movie was to keep them occupied while we are talking."

"I see, well I will tell your Dad and start the movie in the RV. Your Dad and I talked everything over last night. Junior can you please come in the RV I have an ice cream cone for you."

"Yes, Nana coming!" he replied. He opened the RV door and went inside.

Nana came out and sat by Papa. Katrina looked at her parents.

"Since the children are busy eating their ice cream cones and watching the movie you rented. Your mom and I discussed what you told us yesterday evening. We agree that it is for the best if Wayne stays with us. I made some phone calls to Phoenix this morning to check on what appointments that was scheduled. We made some changes so we can be here, however I will need to fly to Phoenix and make some more necessary changes. How is Junior doing with everything that happened?" Floyd took Katrina hand in his while they talked.

"Mom and Dad are you sure about this because I don't want you to regret the decision in the future. You both will be giving up a lot and your plans for retirement will be put on hold. I am not sure how long it will last." She knew that their decision was a big one and she didn't know how she would pay them back.

"We are sure and we will be there no matter what. We will be there for you and the rest of the family. Junior is having difficulty understanding why he cannot see his brother, since he did not do anything wrong." Floyd was sad about his grandchildren and was going to be there for them.

"Dad maybe this summer while you are spending time with Junior he will open up and talk to you about Wayne. I am worried about him. I have already scheduled an appointment with Dr. McDoodle, because he is wetting the bed again and is having anger issues."

"Why doesn't Junior stay the night here and we will bring him home tomorrow? This way him and Papa can go fishing early tomorrow morning when it is not as hot and humid."

"Mom that a good idea. Why don't you and Dad come over to the house for dinner then for a cook out? Dean will be home and he can throw some hamburgers and hot dogs on the grill." Katrina was glad that her parents' were here, but she still was questioning everything.

"We will visit for a while but I want to leave at dusk so I can get Rosa home for a bath and into bed. I will give you a calendar with all the current court dates and appointments with the counselors when you come for dinner."

They stayed at the campground all afternoon. The movie was over and Katrina helped her mom make dinner. The kids wanted macaroni and cheese with hot dogs. These days that was all they would eat. She was cutting up green onions to put into a macaroni salad. She wasn't eating a lot these days because her stomach was always hurting. She was sure it was the stress she had been under for the past month or so. Floyd had a campfire started to cook the hot dogs on a special type of fork. He was helping Junior put his hot dog on it. It was going to be a warm night and it had been weeks since they had any rain in the area. She could not believe how fast the day had gone by and the sun was at the horizon.

"Junior how would you like to stay the night with Nana and Papa tonight?"

"Can I mom that would really be neat!" Junior stated in a happy way.

"mom how come I cannot stay too." Rosa had a pout face and her hands were folded in front of her chest.

"Rosa you can stay with Nana and Papa tomorrow night. Nana and Papa are coming over for dinner and you can go back with them for the night." She answered her daughter.

"But for right now you are going home with me. Say good bye and good night to Nana and Papa." Katrina helped with putting the extra food away and took the garbage in back of the van. They would drop it off at the dumpster next to the office. They needed to stop there anyway to drop off the movie and pass.

Rosa gave Papa a hug then Nana. "Good night Papa and Nana, see you tomorrow."

"Bye mom and dad we will see you tomorrow for dinner. Junior be a good boy and listen to your grandparents. Good luck with the fishing in the morning. We will see you tomorrow night." She said.

"Bye mom sees you tomorrow." He was excited that he was staying the night and then going fishing with Papa in the morning. Junior went inside the RV and started to set up where he was sleeping.

She gave her mom and dad a hug. "Thanks again mom and dad for everything," then went to catch up with Rosa that was standing next to the van waiting for the door to be unlocked.

Katrina unlocked all the doors and helped Rosa into the booster in the back seat. She had a lot to do in the morning starting with phone calls. She knew some of the places would be closed since it was a Saturday however she would leave a message so they could return the call first thing Monday. She was driving home the same way she came from the campground. She needed to call the insurance company that carried their home owner's policy. She also needed to try to remember where she put the VHS tape that explained where babies came from. She had bought it for the kids to watch, since their Aunt was having a baby. She wanted to review first to make sure that it was appropriate. But that did not happen since she caught the children watching it unsupervised. She thought she had donated it to a single father's group along with other baby items. She had to get on the Internet to see if they could find the video now that it was brought up in court. She also had to make copies of the court information that they had received for her parents.

She had so much on her mind these days it was hard to see Wayne every time they went to the court house. She was sure she was going to have mental breakdown. She felt alone as her private life with Dean was put under a microscope. She was starting to second guess every decision she was making now and what she did in the past when it came to her parental skills. She was a mother, a lover, a wife and a women but she was not sure who Katrina was anymore. It did not matter to the attorneys or the court system that Prue and her family was close in declaring bankruptcy. She had manipulated the court system in her favor by using such an opportune time with just two sentences in Cassandra's diary. They would get their necessary money for financial support once the civil suit was over and they weren't even going to have a trial. Katrina did not think of it at the time she was still distraught about everything. She was almost home and Rose and fallen asleep. She still had a lot of questions and no one would give her the answer.

THE DAYS OF going back and forth to the Lazy J Campground was taking its toll. Floyd would leave in the morning to return to the Phoenix area to get a few of their personal things done and then he would return to stay for another two weeks. Her parents had decided to go to the next town over to hook up the RV at another campground. The Crooked Bend Campground was near a river. The kids weren't able to go fishing but they had hayrides on the weekends and family bingo on Sunday afternoons. The other issue was that Rosa and Junior could see their grandparents but no longer stay the night. The summer was going by quickly and school would start in six weeks. Floyd was now officially the guardian of Wayne. Since court dates went from one month to the next even with cancellations. Her dad had asked her to help look for an apartment that was affordable. Dean had been looking for a used third car with low payments. If Katrina's mom had to stay she would need a vehicle and ones it was paid off it would be the kid's car once they received their license.

The summer days went quickly by filled with court dates, counseling along with traveling back and forth to the campgrounds. The day had approached for Katrina to do a deposition. Her lawyer wanted to speak to her before going into the conference room; she was nervous that morning and could not even eat a light breakfast.

The court recorder was set up at the rectangle table in the back as the attorneys took a seat. Katrina took a seat at across from Prue's attorney. The deposition was going to be recorded by Ms. Malone. The document stated the following:

Mrs. Katrina Garrett taken this case is on the behalf of the plaintiffs before Samantha Malone, Certified Shorthand Reporter, Registered Professional Reporter, and Notary Republic, at 10:15 a.m., on February 14, in the law offices of Santiago, Lawson, O'Harey, and LLC. 645 West Salem Street, Suite 765 A, St. James, Illinois.

Appearances were: Mr. Vinnie S. Santiago representing the plaintiff, Mr. Jack Steward representing Wayne Garrett, and Ms. Jammie Weatherspoon representing Katrina Garrett.

"Let the record reflect this is the discovery disposition of Katrina Garrett taken pursuant to notice and the Illinois Rules of Civil Procedure. Mrs. Garrett my name is Vinnie Santiago. I represent Cassandra and Prue in this lawsuit. I'm going to be asking you some questions about your knowledge of the facts pertinent to this case. I assume you have never done this before, am I correct?

Katrina looked at him and responding with a, "Yes, sir".

"Your attorney may have gone over the rules, but I want to explain them to you again. It is important to try to follow these rules as best as you can. This way it is when the court reporter types up the transcript of this deposition. The information that you have been trying to convey to us is very clear and that we can understood it and that it will not be too vague." Attorney Santiago was waiting for a reply from her.

"Yes," was all she replied?

"The court reporter types up the transcript of this deposition and the information that you have been conveying to us is said very clear along with understanding what is said. We don't want anything said ambiguous during this deposition. Okay?" Santiago stated.

She replied, "Yes sir I understand."

"Then we will proceed. The first rule is to answer all the questions out loud and use words that the general public understands. The word Yes is okay to use or using the word okay but the word uh-huh/ huh-uh cannot be used. Can you do that?" Mr. Santiago stated.

She replied, "Yes".

"Finally, the most important, if I ask you a question that you don't understand, please tell me to repeat it or rephrase it. Can you do that?" Mr. Santiago continued asking her this form of questions for over two hours.

She replied again with a, "yes".

"If this happens, remember that it is not your fault but mine. My job is to ask simpler questions about the case that are easy to understand and not ambiguous. Please remind me if I don't do this. All right?"

She replied, "Yes."

"Katrina Garrett, having been first duly sworn, was examine and testified as follows:" The examination questions Mr. Santiago began, How old are you, ma'am? How long have you been married? Where are you from originally?"

"When did you come to the Belvidere area? When did you meet Mr. and Mrs.

How far did you go in school? Have you worked outside the home? I am going to show you exhibit A can you tell me what it is?"

She replied, "I am 40 years old and was married in 1985. I met my husband in high school. I graduated high school and then went to college. Unfortunately, I did not graduate college and I am currently enrolled at a community college. My husband and I moved into the Belvidere area in 1996. We lived here for several years until the house across the street was built. This is where Ms. Prue moved into sometime in 1999. Our families became friends until this incident occurred. I hope that this answers all your questions, Mr. Santiago."

"No because you have not answered the question pertaining to exhibit A, would you like me to repeat the questions?"

"I am sorry, exhibit A is a family calendar that I hang on our refrigerator. I usually write important appointments, but I sometimes put on the calendar if the weather is unusual or the name of the person that has the appointment." I sometimes write things down in a notebook or Journal." She responded.

"Thank you for clarifying exhibit A for me, now to move forward with the examination about the given day in question around May eighth. Does this date have any importance, Katrina?" Mr. Santiago was writing information down on a piece of paper.

"Yes, it is the day I went to a yearly banquet and my friend Bobby Jo picked me up for. Wayne was watching his younger siblings until my husband Dean came home from work. He was running late and would be home forty minutes after I left. The reason I can tell you this is I called him on his cell phone."

"Do you know that the allegations against you are for neglect because your son Wayne was unsupervised especially around minors since he portrays inappropriate sexual behavior," Mr. Santiago had more notes in front of him.

She was beginning to get tired and was hoping that this circus would end soon. Mr. Santiago seemed to have only some facts about the giving day. She wanted to know if anyone mentioned that while Wayne was watching his siblings that she had sent Cassandra home when she left with Bobby Jo. Why was Cassandra back in their house when the house rules were that no one was allowed in the house when parents' were not home. Yet, no one bothered to find out and all that Katrina wanted was to know the truth. The facts had already been distorted by the stories that the children had gave verbally in their depositions. The reports and documents that are completed had not matched the stories or versions of what happened by the children. Katrina did not understand why Rosa, Danaka, Cassandra and others had different stories. The facts were harder to find, so the depositions were slowly being found by Judge MacGuire has being the most important material for the case.

The court had subpoena records from physicians, the elementary school and the middle school. The civil lawsuit was for negligent and suing her for the complete cost in her and Dean's home owner's policy of $300,000.00 or a substantial settlement that everyone agreed on without a jury trial. The deposition was over and in two hours Douglas Skinner a friend of the Garrett's would be here for his deposition. Katrina would be able to go home. The depositions needed for the case was just about done and then it would be decided to go in front of the judge for a bench trial or jury trial. Katrina wanted all of it to go away. She had answered the plaintiff's complaint at Law Proof of Service. The months went quickly and there were times she did not remember what day it was. The temperatures were cooling down and the leaves on the surrounding trees were changing to their brilliant hues of yellow, orange or reds. Telling everyone that fall was here and winter would be here soon. Wayne would stay at the correctional for juveniles for three months and her parents would drive the RV back to the southwest to store it for the winter. Once this was done, her mother Ruthanne would fly back and stay in the apartment just north of where Katrina and Dean lived. Dean would now be financial liable for two families, attorney fees, and counseling for everyone that would need it by court rules. If Wayne had a good week he was allowed to visit on the weekend as long as Ruthanne and Floyd could supervise. Katrina was stripped of all parental rights. The counseling sessions were for Rosa and Wayne to discuss what they did wrong and the consequences. Rosa started to eat junk food in her room and soon was showing an eating disorder. Wayne was released to live in a farm house for boys so counseling would begin for him. Dean had visited him there several times and was teaching him to drive. Katrina did not like what the state did and now was considered to be uncooperative in counseling. The judge and state attorney kept saying this was for Wayne's best interest, but she was beginning to question everything and was ignored. This year during the holidays Wayne would travel with Floyd and Ruthanne to visit Ruthanne's younger sister Trudy. Trudy lived near the Kentucky, Tennessee line with her husband Colton. They would be there for a few days and return back to their apartment.

Katrina was tired of the harassment that Rosa had to deal with. She had gone to the elementary school to talk to the principal about an incident that another student had done in the girl's bathroom. The extracurricular activities for Rosa would be volleyball, field track, and band. She was taking out of swimming and ice skating to avoid any other harassment by other students that were associated with Cassandra.

Dean and Katrina had decided at this time to get the children home together, they would need to move. They wanted to be close enough for their children to keep their friends. While Wayne was at the farm house and her parents returned to their home in Tucson, she was back to the drinking starting sometime in the morning.

One of Katrina's friend's Jessica currently worked as a paralegal for Attorney Jack Steward. Jessica's husband worked as a sheriff in another suburb and was hardly home. Dean and Katrina started to do family activities with them. They had gone to a state park to go camping and fishing. Jessica's daughters Emily and Meltilda played with Rosa. Meltilda but everyone called her by the nickname Tillie. Tillie and Rosa were best friends. Dean, Katrina, Junior and Rosa would go to Jessica's house for dinner, to drink and watch football on the very large flat screen television.

This week however they would be at their house to have family game night. Katrina had already had more than her share of Bloody Mary's or Irish whiskey to drink. When Jessica arrived she had brought another bottle of hard liquor to share. Katrina grabbed the wine glasses and told Jessica to put on her swimsuit. The hor d'oeuvres had already been made and was in the refrigerator for the time being. Jessica changed into her swimsuit along with Katrina. They were going down into the Florida room where a six person Jacuzzi was located. The college finals were over and it was time to relax until spring semester.

"Jessica next week the house will be put on the local real estate market and I will be busy boxing up things we are not currently using to be put into storage. The storage unit we rented is just across the street so if you could help by putting boxes into your van to take over there I would appreciate the help." She waited for a response.

"Katrina I can help in the evenings after work, but do you think Wayne will come home if you move."

"I hope so, Junior is really having anxiety attacks and the psychiatrist has put him on a different type of prescription to help with depression."

"Katrina I found two houses that are for sale over by where I live. I brought the information with me so you can call the real estate agent if you are interested and can call them to make an appointment." Jessica stated as she sipped on her drink.

"Thank you for all your help during these difficult times, Jessica." Katrina had already finished her drink and was pouring another glass. I have a favor to ask you. Is it possible for you to watch Rosa next Tuesday for a couple of hours?"

"I do not see why not, what is going on?" Jessica grabbed a towel to dry off and sit in the chair.

"I have a doctor appointment with an orthopedic because my knee is bothering me. The Jacuzzi helps but I noticed that it is swollen. It hurts when I walk on it. We also sold this house and the new owners will be here in three weeks. Dean and I have not looked for a new home since we did not think it would sell especially during the holiday season. Now we need to look and find one that is empty. Do you have any suggestions?"

"No Katrina the only two houses, one of the houses' I found still have people living in them." Jessica left the Florida room to get the information on houses for sale.

Katrina slowly got up and out of the Jacuzzi and dried herself off. She had picked up numerous boxes and gave to the Goodwill Center. She had been taking small boxes over to the storage unit. She would talk with a local real estate agent and get her busy looking for houses that fit the criteria. The only wish she had currently was to have everyone home, but the courts constantly changed their minds about releasing Wayne. They also changed the date for Rosa to visit her brother except in counseling. Rosa and Danaka had to go to the Chance Bailey Center for evaluation or interview for victims. This was ordered by the States Attorney as part of the investigation into Wayne's sexual misconduct. She knew was vindictive but this had gone too far and why was she trying to ruin her family. She had done nothing to hurt Prue or Cassandra to cause this reaction. The court dates seemed to blur together along with the counseling. Katrina had plenty to do. She decided to go back to college to achieve an associate degree in the arts by attending in class part-time, moving, volleyball for Rosa, Junior chess club, and anything to keep her mind busy. She had decided to work part-time as a person delivering phone books in the rural communities. The next issue Katrina had to deal with was Rosa's eating disorder, Junior and Dean's depression and Katrina's physical limitations. She had gone to see the orthopedic physician and took ex-rays. The area behind the knee was swollen and discolored. The orthopedic physician, Kolby Douglas took a long needle and stuck into the knee to try to drain it. This method did not help and he decided to put a cortisone medicine in it and he would see her in two weeks. It would give her some time to heal and get back unto her feet. The x-rays had shown that the muscle ACL was gone and surgery would be needed to replace it. Dr. Douglas scheduled the surgery at the hospital in two weeks. She pre-registered so that the necessary documentation would be completed through their insurance. After the surgery Dr. Douglas would give her a cast on the entire leg. She would not be able to walk for two more weeks since it was not a walking cast. She had contacted her college professors and the attorneys'. Judge McGuire was upset about the whole idea and requested written documentation from the hospital and Dr. Douglas. Katrina was to take time to heal but the judge found that she was being hostile. The courts decided to dismiss with prejudice Katrina's, Rosa's, and two other depositions. However, the findings of the attorneys' would be against Wayne and Katrina. She did not understand all the judicial terms. Mr. Santiago's office had a document sent to everyone involved in the civil case including the Olympia Fields settlement demand letter during the 1945 court case. The home owner insurance company and Ms. Weatherspoon wanted a quick settlement so that she could move into the house. The house was smaller square footage but did come with a full size pool and deck in the back yard. The house was being sold by owner who was getting married and his new wife already had a house.

They went to a bank to finalize the paper work to show the home being sold. She had to move around on crutches for several more weeks but Bobby Jo and her family helped them get moved in. She only had a knee brace on now so driving and errands were still a chore but now she had some freedom. She had found a wellness counselor only twenty minutes from home so she could get some emotional therapy. She felt it was time before another incident took place and depression paid its toll. A few weeks ago while driving to a doctor appointment she was behind a semi-trailer truck. She was upset about the justice system and the crooked people that were dictating the outcomes of lives. She at one moment thought about taking her life by ramming her vehicle into the semi-truck under carriage. She was wandering how the family would survive or who would come to the funereal.

The other time was when she had been drinking excessively and took one of her sharp steak knives so that she could cut her wrist. Dean interfered and took the knife away from her. Fortunately she had not cut her wrist to deep and it looked like a scratch. Judge McGuire had put out to the plaintiff and defendant that a motion to Quash Proof of. A status report and depositions were moved out by three more weeks on the court calendar. The counselor decided that Rosa was not opening up and asked family members to talk with her about honesty. The first thing she would be told that there was not a real Easter Bunny or Santa Clause, that it was mom and dad playing the fantasy. This broke Rosa's heart and Katrina knew the next year it would be hard for Rosa to accept this. The next obstacle that she would have to deal with was Rosa would need to go up to the podium to testify about what happened with her and Cassandra while Katrina was gone on that specific day. She would need to be honest with her answers and she would need to do it in front of the judge, attorneys, Wayne, Nana, Papa and everyone that would be in the court room.

The states attorney would call another witness to be heard besides hearing Prue on the stand. Judge McGuire would then here closing arguments from both sides. Katrina felt like a criminal as a stay at home mom that neglected her children and was wrongly accused of sexually abusing her sons. The proof of her was what Wayne had said during consoling that a women had inappropriately touched him The court had asked Katrina to confess to the charge and then no harm would come to her except that she never touched her sons or any other children in that manner.

The states attorney calls Ms Longhorn to the stand.

"Ms. Longhorn where do you live currently?"

"I live diagonal from Prue's house and three houses down from the Garrett's house." She replied.

"Can you please tell us what you heard on that day in May," Cobra wanted to close the case and prosecute Katrina in the fullest allowed by the law.

Katrina felt sick to her stomach as the questioning continued. She listened in disbelief about the charges that the court wanted to charge her. She felt like she was watching everything in slow motion. This woman on the stand known as Miss Longhorn she never met and only saw her a few times in her yard. Yet, she told the court room that she heard foul language and loud talking on the drive way of her house. She pointed her finger toward Katrina's children and their attorney's. She stated, these young men and others were playing basketball in the drive-way and yelling profanity for everyone to hear." When Prue was on the stand she started weeping and shaking her head.

"Please state your name for the record," said the honorable MacGuire.

"My name is Prudence Hallow, but my best friends call me Prue."

"Will you please tell the court why you are here?"

"I am here to make sure justice is done for my young daughter Cassandra," Prue replied as a Kleenex is used to wipe her tears on her cheek. Prue began telling the court room how her best friend allowed her daughter Cassandra to get hurt.

"I tried talking to Katrina about what happened at her house on a number of occasions and that I did not want my children at her house. A best friend would listen and possibly do something about it. I was just diagnosed with cancer and the doctors currently do not know how long I have to live." Prue began crying harder.

Katrina knew that this was just a way for Prue to get money and pull her family down to where she could lose everything that mattered to her.

Katrina watched Prue but she knew that whatever happened that the real justice would come to those that wait. Katrina was willing to wait as long as she needed to so her family would be once again together. The states attorney was up for re-election and would use any means to show the public that the State's Attorney's Office had a specific agenda for parents that neglected or abused their children.

As they exited the courtroom, her parents' were waiting along with close friends and a minister from the church which they belonged to for many years. Pastor Abraham and Pastor Jacob were next to Katrina's parents' the Peabody's.

"How are you doing Katrina?" asked Pastor Jacob

Before she answered. Katrina felt light headed and things began to turn she took the next step and then everything went blank. She had passed out. Luckily Pastor Abraham caught her as she took the next step and was caught with open arms. Pastor Abraham and Pastor Jacob finished escorting her down the stairs and outside so she could get some fresh air.

"Are you all right?" Pastor Jacob was still holding her hand a she found a park bench.

Pastor Abraham will be over in a few minutes he wanted to talk to Dean. Pastor Jacob handed her a water bottle.

"Now drink this slowly and take some sow deep breathes." Pastor Jacob was trying to calm her down.

"I am sorry Pastor Jacob, I am just at a loss and there are so many things happening around me." She wiped her tears away with a Kleenex she had tucked in her purse.

"Pastor Jacob, how is she doing?" Pastor Abraham looked at her.

"Pastor Jacob and I do have some sad news and we are sorry that we cannot be here for the end of the court days. However, the new pastor will be at the church if you need to talk to someone." Pastor Jacob slowly got up from the park bench and stood next to Pastor Abraham. She looked at both of them and was not sure what to say.

"Katrina, I gave Dean the address of the new church that I will be preaching at if you need to get a hold of me." Pastor Abraham stated. Pastor Jacob looked at Katrina, "My new preaching job has me starting after the county fair in August. So my family and I can get moved in before school started.

Katrina was trying to understand why God was abandoning her and her family at a time in need.

"Okay so do you know who the new minister for the church will be?" Katrina was still sniffling but had started to get her composer back.

Pastor Jacob replied, "It is a young family from another small town and the new minister is a women. That is all I know at this time.

"Thank you for everything, Pastor Jacob and Pastor Abraham for being there for our family." She gave each of them a hug and slowly walked toward the van. He drove them home and dropped Katrina off at the house to finish

Dean opened the door to the van and helped Katrina into the front seat. Dean was worried about Katrina's mental state and her health. She looked tired most days and he wanted to comfort her. Yet, Dean did not want to argue with her about taking better care of herself. He was actual glad that his wife was back taking college classes and going to the community college.

Thinking to herself, how I wish I could go somewhere and scream at the world. However, she knew if she did this then people would think she was having a mental break down and then what would happen to her children. While, Dean went to pick up the children at Bobby Jo's she would take a hot shower and try to relax. She had turned on the television to listen to the evening news. Since, the terrorists attacks on 9/11 the United States had deployed a number of troops to the Middle East, the economy currently had not rebounded like the government wanted and people they knew had foreclosed on their house. The question being asked by the public was it getting close to be the end of the world. This bothered

Katrina along with what had been going on with her family. Things had definitely changed and more changes would be done by the government in the hope to protect the American people. The regulations at international airports would have people go through a scan along with all personal items to make sure no weapons would be brought aboard the commercial airlines. There were restrictions on what was allowed on board and no meals were served if you wanted to fly within the United States. Everyone was required to have a photo ID and many government office buildings also had electronic scanners to make sure no weapons could be brought inside the buildings...

She took a quick shower because the next part of the news was telling the listening area about a tropical storm in the Atlantic Ocean that would become a hurricane. June first was the start of Hurricane season and the meteorologist were worried about this tropical storm that was heading toward the Florida coastline. She sat down on the corner of the bed to listen to the report from another T.V. channel. The only reason that this caught her attention was because she had several great aunts, cousins, and family that lived close to the Gulf of Mexico. It was August 29, 2005; the projection of the tropical storm was to gain strength make land fall again along the coast of Louisiana, Mississippi, or Texas. Katrina would need to talk to her parent's to ask them if everyone was alright and if her great aunt and uncle had actually left their home to get away from the storm. Dean, Junior and Rosa had just gotten home. She would call her parent's first thing in the morning to see if they had heard from family members.

"Junior, please go get your pajamas on tomorrow you have school. Rosa you need to take our bath and get to bed. Maybe I can have you read from one of the books before saying good night."

She would watch the news again at 10 o'clock p.m. and then get to bed. The evening went by quickly and Dean had already turned the television back on. The T.V. stations had announced that a state of emergency was taking place along the gulf coast. The tropical storm had been named Katrina and it had reached the Gulf of Mexico. In the Gulf tropical storm Katrina was now a major hurricane classified in category 5 and was heading toward New Orleans. Katrina watched as the Hurricane Katrina came closer to land. She hoped that family members had taken the mandatory evacuation. The natural disaster would be one of the worst storms to hit the

United States in a long time. The news people that were down there would update and show photos of the damaged areas. She continues to watch and would go on the Internet to see about the devastation. The Louisiana governor and Mississippi governor asked the federal government program known as FEMA had sent people, along with the National Guard, and the Red Cross would make a plea for the nation to pull together to help those in need. The response was greater than the Red Cross expected and along with monetary donations people from the other states started their journey to help others get back on their feet. The hope of rebuilding was the only decision made by people that wanted to live by the beach.

"Dean I want our family to donate a monetary to the Red Cross there is so much devastation in those southern states." She watched the news program as new photos of the area were being broadcasted.

"How much should we donate?" was Dean's replied.

Katrina called the 800 number for the Red Cross and punched in her Visa Credit Card nine digits for the donation. Then she hung up the phone. Dean had already turned off the television and headed toward the master bedroom.

The next morning the sun was shining bright through the living room bay window.

She waited until late morning to call her Dad.

Her great aunt and uncle lived near the Bay of St. Louis and Gulfport Mississippi and the other great aunt lives north of Baton Rouge.

"Good morning sweetheart, No I know that they left during the evacuation and if I hear anything else I will call you." Floyd replied to his daughter's worry.

"It will probably be weeks before phone service or electric will be completely restored so try to be patient."

"How is everyone?" Katrina wanted to keep the phone conversation short. She still had to get ready for another family counseling meeting where Wayne was now living. The judge had decided that Junior and Rosa could stay with Katrina and Dean. This way Floyd and Ruth Ann could return their life in Arizona.

"Your mom and I are fine. How are you holding up after we moved from the apartment? How are the children doing? Are they getting ready for the school year to begin?"

"We put most of the furniture from the apartment in the basement where Dean is putting up dry wall to make the boys a large bedroom and full bathroom. The judge has not given us the answer but Wayne coming home. The judge told us that if we corroborate and the counseling is going well then maybe by Christmas Wayne could come home to live. We have a family session this evening. Rosa and Junior have all their school supplies and have a half day tomorrow. I will call you this weekend to give you an update. I love you Dad. Bye."

"I love you too and will talk with you in a couple of days. This way the children can tell us about the new school." Katrina heard a click as her Dad hung up the phone.

She had to go pick up Junior and Rosa from school then get them ready to leave for the family session. Dean was already on his way home from the office. Her college classes had started last week and she went to the community college twice a week.

She had everyone ready when Dean pulled into the drive way

They arrived at the building for the family counseling on time. They sat down at a small round table in a room that looked like a school cafeteria. A middle age women came over to the table.

'Hello, Garrett Family. My name is Stacy Green, I am here to take the children to another room while you discuss with the psychologist any concerns before the regular counseling."

"Junior and Rosa go with Ms Green she has some toys you can play with in the other room. Then we will come and get you when it is your turn."

"Okay mom, Rosa and Junior replied almost in unison, as they followed Ms Green.

Once the children left two middle-aged men and young women came into the room.

"Good evening," as one of the gentlemen began the conversation. My name is Doctor Evan Scott this is my colleague Janice Blaze." My name is Tom Klondike; I am in charge of the academics here. They all took a seat next to Katrina and Dean.

"The reason we want to talk with you first is because during Wayne's private counseling sessions something came up and we are concerned about the safety of the children." Doctor Scott was talking in a monotone manner." Katrina you do understand we are only looking out for the children."

Katrina was alert and listening as he spoke.

"Wayne has been having some disturbing dreams and it is about him being sexual abused by a women." We think it is you Katrina. Have you had sexual contact with Wayne?"

Katrina's mouth dropped. "What are you talking about? Why would I have sexual contact with Wayne and not with both sons? And furthermore that is downright disgusting. I would never touch my sons in that manner. Unless you talking about when they were infants or toddlers changing diapers or giving them baths is considered sex abuse. That means that ever parent has to be punished because of changing a dirty diaper." Katrina's voice had risen to almost yelling at them.

"We understand that Wayne looks like your husband. All you have to do is tell us what you did sexually to Wayne and we won't press charges." Doctor Scott was waiting for her to answer.

"You are telling me if I admit doing sex with my son nothing going to happen, really. I cannot admit to something I did when I didn't do it in the first place." Katrina watched as the man named Tom got up from the chair next to her. She noticed how tall he was and he had a sports jacket that matched his jeans.

"Excuse me I will go and get Wayne now. He should be done with some of his studies and chores." then he walked through one of the other doors into a hall way.

Katrina was upset and could not belief that they were asking such ludicrous questions.

Dean looked at her and Katrina felt like a caged animal.

"My wife has never touched any of our children sexual or physically abused them. I don't know where you people get this weird and sick idea from. However you might want to look again at your notes or maybe Wayne is trying to manipulate you Doctor Scott." Dean replied more calming than she did.

Katrina would finish this counseling session but it would be her last. She didn't care to talk to these doctors that manipulate and accuse innocent people especially her.

Doctor Scott was busy writing notes on a pad of paper. Katrina was angry and she wanted to leave. Katrina could tell that Dr. Scott didn't like people that lied and individual's that abused children he despised. Katrina knew no matter what she said now would only make matters worse.

Dr. Scott looked at her and she felt like he was looking through her.

"Dean Can you tell us why Wayne would say that your wife his mother would do such terrible things?" Doctor Scott was writing down more notes. Katrina was getting sick to her stomach.

"My wife told you it wasn't her and I have no reason to doubt her with the answer she gave you earlier." Dean responded

The door opened and Wayne entered the room and took a seat by Doctor Scott.

Katrina looked at her son. He looked good and had grown a little since the last visit.

"Wayne tells your parent's what you told me about the dream you keep having."

"Okay, I guess. I see a woman like my mom over me unfastening my pants and touching places that shouldn't be touched. Then I wake up."

"Wayne why would you say that; that is disgusting and grose.Could it of been one of the teenager baby sitters a long time ago or a house that you went over to play at."

"Can I please have sheet of paper and a pencil or pen? I will give you a list of babysitter names and the houses that he went over to play with their children." She began writing the names down then handed the list to him. Since you have nothing better to do but accuse me why don't you check into these individuals that might have touched my son inappropriately." She said with confidence. Doctor Scott took the list and put it with the note pad. Katrina had only met Dr. Scott one other time outside the courtroom and now she knew why she didn't like him. Dr. Scott was scrawny looking compared to most men and cunning when it came to trying to find out the truth through mind games. He wore thick glasses and dressed business casual. He was arrogant and self-centered when talking to women. He consistently degraded women and felt that he was better than most people that the judicial system sent him. Katrina's mom also felt that he didn't like women when they had taken Wayne to his office downtown for counseling.

Dean looked at his wife, then his son. He knew with these allegations his wife would no longer talk to any of them. She would keep it all inside and uncooperative in any other counseling sessions.

The woman at the table was a parolee officer and there waiting for her to claim that she abused or neglected her children. Except she had never done anything to her children and especially the disgusting charges now they were trying to charge her for. Since she didn't proclaim that she was guilty of the charges the woman stood up and walk out of the room.

"Really, you think I would touch you that way Wayne. I find that not only disgusting but appalled by the thought of it." She was saddened by his dreams. The family session was lasting longer than first believed and the children had not been together for months.

"I only have one last thing to say to you Dr. Scott, I think what you have said and accused me of is totally disgusting. Why would I do such things to one son and not the other? Your explanation is that is because Wayne looks like my husband."

"Now I think Junior and Rosa should join us for only a few minutes and I will leave the area. Dean, will you stay with the children?" "I don't trust Dr. Scott or anyone here to be alone with our children." she slowly got up from the hard chair and walked toward the door. The young woman in her thirties with such a caring qualities brought Junior and Rosa into the room.

"Mommy, where are you going?" Rosa pulled away and ran toward her.

"It is okay Mommy will be outside and waiting for you. Go spend some time with your brothers and then we will go home." She smile at the children and went outside. She was only praying to have her family together just in time for the Christmas holidays.

She looked through the glass of the door to watch Junior and Wayne start talking about school but Rosa had climb into the chair next to Dean. She was only watching while her brothers talked about the latest Nintendo game. Then she turned away and walked toward a picnic table that was on the side of the old farm house that the state had made for boys of all ages that were being investigated for abuse or abusive environments. She started to cry and made herself a promise not to let the children see her. Next week she would call the health insurance support line to find help for her to overcome the suicidal thoughts she had been having along with the depression. She wanted someone to talk to and not to be placed on all kinds of anti depression medicine. She thought to herself.

"I need to be alert for the next few months and strong for Rosa and Junior. Wayne now was out of her control but maybe if Judge MacGuire and attorney's see she was now getting help too then by Christmas Wayne would come home. It would be a nice surprise."

It felt like it was hours before Dean, Junior, and Rosa came out to look for her. Dean handed her a small card with the next family session listed along with the next court date which was scheduled for September 23, 2005 and a memo at the bottom requesting the VHS that the children watched about where Babies comes from. She snickered at the request.

They got into the van and headed home.

"Junior how was your visit with Wayne?" she looked over her shoulder into the passenger van seats.

"Mom, it was great the lady said that I can come and visit him again in a few weeks. That the judge would let me if I did my counseling too."

"Rosa did you visit too?" She looked at her daughter through a mirror on the sun visor.

"Mommy he has grown so tall I did not know what to say to him so I sat next to daddy." Rosa grabbed her doll that was next to her and held it now in her arms.

Dean had not said a word since they left.

"Do you believe the gull they had to assume that Wayne's dream was me? And the biggest joke was to have me admit to sexual abuse of my son and yet the state would not press charges if I admitted to it. Really how sickening. How could any mother or person do what they suggest to their child is beyond me. I am not going to admit to something that I did not do in the first place." She was still angry at the suggestion and now the defense attorney or judge wants the ridiculous VHS tape. Which by the way, I think I donated several years ago to a shelter because my younger sister had her children." She was quiet for the rest of the way home.

"Babe tomorrow I will look for the VHS tape and the filing cabinets to see if I donated it to the shelter with the rest of the infant clothes. Is there anything else I need to do?"

Dean was trying to understand but he was worried about the ongoing cost of lawyer fees, court fees, and now more medical for mental health.

The entire family was now in counseling with different psychologist or psychiatrist because of depression.

"No Katrina that will help and you should work on studying for the upcoming midterm in your business management class." Dean replied.

"Do you know why they want the VHS tape and do you know that Wayne and Junior had figured out a back door on the computer that went around the firewalls. Apparently, while we were in bed Junior and Wayne would get onto the computer then get onto a web page so they could see porno sites." Dean wants to know if she knew this.

"I knew that Wayne would get on the computer and went on various web sites for research on a topic for his history class, but porno, I didn't know. She answered in a low voice. It was late when they finally got home. Dean carried Rosa into the house. Junior grabbed his little toy bag and followed. Katrina went into the house. She had noticed that the communication between her and Dean were shaky. She was wandering if he did not believe her when she told him that she had not touched Wayne. On the other hand, did he really think she was not watching their children or their friends that came to the house to play? Did he think that she was a neglect parent? She was emotionally stressed. Katrina would worry about trying to talk to him another time since most of the time these days all they did was argue.

Dean had already gone to bed. She needed a strong drink. She went into her side of the closet to find her secret stash of Tequila. She opened the bottle and took two long gulps. The liquor burned her throat as it went down. She would deal with everything tomorrow.

The next day she got up with Junior and Rosa as they got ready for school. They had both began riding the school bus. Once they were on their way to school. She would begin the task of cleaning the house. She noticed that on the answering machine that her mom had called.

She pushed the retrieval button. "You have two new messages."

"Hi Katrina its Mom please call me back. The attorney called last night and told us about some new laws being passed dealing with abuse, neglect and sex cases."

The next message stated," Hello Mrs. Garrett this is your insurance agent and I have found your home owners policy. The defensive attorney has contacted us about the case against you. Please call me so I can discuss with you and or Dean what the insurance company plans to do in settling the case. My number is 1-847-989-5409 extension 3345 and asks for Gary Straite

Katrina was hoping that the day would be filled with good news. Then the phone rang.

"Good morning," she answered.

"Katrina, have we received in bills or statements from the attorney's office?" Dean wanted to move some money out of the CDS that he had set aside for each child as college money.

"Yes Dean we have received a statement from the county clerk's office for court fees, why are you asking?' She replied.

"I will need to take some of Wayne's college money and Rosa's CD to help with the finances. Plus some of the guys I work with are being laid off or have been given a choice to take early retirement. I have a meeting I need to go to and I will be home late tonight. I have already written on my computer calendar the upcoming counseling, of Wayne's session and court dates. Bye" Katrina heard the dial tone from the telephone.

She was glad that he was working late again. She would do her homework after Rosa and Junior went to bed. She had found the information about VHS tape and she did donate it like she said and had gone onto a web site to find one that was similar to it. She would e-mail Dean the information so he could order it on line.

Unfortunately, the days and weeks went quickly. Katrina's dad, Floyd had called for an update about her great aunt and uncle.

"Hi Dad, is there any news?" she was hoping for good news today.

"Hi Katrina, we heard from great aunt Blanch. They have some electric and are currently living on the property where the house once stood in a fifth wheeler. They lost everything and the area still has the National Guard to help police the area. Have you talked with your mom, yet? The reason is the parole officer and attorney has contacted us. Apparently in January 2006 new laws will be implemented for neglected and sexual abused children. I am not sure why this important except Wayne might not be coming home."

"Dad, why would the judge place him into the foster care system? When you and mom are his guardians? Then leave Rosa and Junior at home."

"Sis I am not sure what it means but you should contact the attorney soon and find out?"

"Dad I would like to thank you and mom for everything. I know we have talked about letting Wayne come to Arizona during his junior year in high school. This way he could apply to the college or university that had aeronautics and astrology school this way he could receive in state university cost and financial aid. Would you mom still be willing to do this if we help by sending money for supporting him

".I will discuss it later with your mom again but we had already agreed on this as a possibility. It is just coming earlier than expected."

"Dad thanks again and I will touch base with you this weekend. Love you. Bye." Katrina hung up the phone. Her eyes were misty from crying and she went into the bedroom.

The news personally was good but she was wandering about the rest of the world. She didn't understand why things were happening like Hurricane Katrina, the suicide bombings, earthquakes and human suffering. So where was the justice in these disasters? However, people that had been such misfortunes always seemed to rebound with hope that tomorrow would be better for everyone. They would rebuild the house with a stronger foundation or their life would be changed to better themselves. Unfortunately right know Katrina wanted her family together and her life back.

On one of the autumn days while Rosa was walking around the block she had heard a strange muffled sound under a bush. She went toward the sound to find a kitten. She would bring home the kitten.

"Mom look what I found hiding under a bush," Rosa said.

"Rosa you know how your dad doesn't like cats of any kind. We need find where the kitten lives. We will post flyers around the area so the owners know that the kitten is safe for now." Katrina did not want Rosa to become attached to the kitten.

"I know that you think you can take care of the kitten but you don't take of Peter," She stated.

"But mom Peter was more the boys pet than mine, plus if I don't find the owner then maybe I can keep it. I promise I will take care of the little guy," said Rosa. Rosa was already trying to think of a name for this tiny yellow ball of fur.

"Mom, we have had the flyers up for a month and no one has contacted us about missing a kitten. Can I please, please keep him I promise I will take care of him," Rosa was smiling and waiting for her answer.

"I suppose Rosa that you can keep the kitten as long as he sleeps in your bedroom. I do not know if Peter and the kitten will get along. Here is an old blanket for him to lie on. Have you picked out a name?" Katrina hesitated about keeping the kitten in the first place. She would talk to Dean about the importance of having Rosa keep the kitten as part of the healing process."

"Mom I have named him Munchy, because he is always eating his food fast from the small bowl," Rosa said cheerfully.

"We will call one of the local vetenarian to make an important so he can get the necessary shots and to make sure that he is a male not a female cat. I will talk with your dad tonight when he comes home from work." Katrina was hoping that Dean would go along with her about keeping the cute yellow Calico.

She had already put Rosa and Junior to bed for the night, Peter was already asleep on the floor by the couch in the living room. When she checked on Rosa, Munchy and curled up next to her. Rosa had begun to go through puberty and was growing up. Rosa still had an eating disorder that caused her to eat junk food in front of the television and piece on in the middle of the night. Katrina had noticed that Munchy and Rosa had a special bond.

"Hi honey you are home and I need to talk to you tonight about something," Katrina watched her husband put the dirty thermos into the sink.

"I am pretty sure that I know what it is about but go ahead and start talking," Dean replied.

"First we received a yellow envelope today that you will need to read and look over. Second I know how you told Rosa that she could not keep the kitten." Katrina stated.

"Okay and so did you find the owner of the kitten," answered Katrina.

"Rosa and I have placed flyers everywhere and it now has been a month. I think with everything that has gone on that Rosa should keep the kitten. It will give her some responsibility of taking care of something and help with the healing process of Wayne leaving for good." Katrina replied.

Dean and I had received a large certified envelope this afternoon from a courier company. She had not opened it because she felt it was bad news and could not face it today. The return address was from the main insurance office in the city. She wanted to wait until Dean came home from work. Yet her curiosity was gnawing at her insides telling her to go ahead and open it. Finally she gave into the urge and opens the envelope carefully to see that it was some kind of document. The opening letter was stating that in the future that the insurance company had the right to deny coverage due to questionable occurrences that had been defined in their home owner's policy. The letter then began to define what was meant by coverage pertaining to personal liability, bodily injury or property damage. Toward the end of the document and letter that if they did not hear from Dean and her that the representative and team manager of the insurance company would continue to handle the claim under the terms given here. She laid the paper on the table so Dean could see it and read it when he got home. She looked inside the large envelope to see if there was anything else only to see another envelope. The business style envelope was not sealed but was addressed to them. It was a letter that the insurance company had received through a Fax machine and a copy was made to give to the Garrett's. The Fax was stating that there would be limited time to respond to the demand letter by Katrina's attorney and waiting for further depositions by Prue's attorney. The depositions were from Prue's psychiatrist and a physician that had seen Cassandra since the case had started. The attorney's would have all the testimonies and could summon consultants from the medical field when they thought it would be necessary for the case. Attorney Vinnie Santiago they stated in the later that the plaintiff Ms Prue should receive fully from the Garrett's home owner policy the amount of $300,000.00 is given to help in any of Cassandra's medical bills and psychiatric care.

She was wandering if this was why the court date had been changed now to October. She hated waiting, but just maybe the October date would be the last to go to court. After two years maybe the unruly case would finally come to an end. Katrina was exhausted and many times wanted to give up. She could remember when Dean and she decided to move out here to live. The only reason they moved out here was to get their children away from the drugs, violence and gangs the larger cities had to contend with all the time. The area was rural, there were plenty of farms and conservation areas for them to enjoy.

However, things change and more people from the cities suburbs were coming out this way and people from the gulf had relocated to north. If this was not enough the States Attorney Morgan Serpentine was to leave because she no longer lived in the area. Her husband that was a lawyer was practicing in a town in the upper part of Wisconsin. The local lawyer took over the position until election time in November.

The attorney that was taking the States Attorney position was a young family man. Katrina had gone with her friend Jessica several times to fund raisers for him. His son was playing on the towns little league team. He was going to run for the office and the fundraisers were going to help his campaign strategy. Katrina would place one of the campaign signs in her yard. The sign stated "Vote for Towering Allan Straits in November Election". Allan was almost 6'6" so everyone had nicknamed him Towering Al. He was committed to the way law and justice was to be given to criminals. On the other hand, he felt family was just as important. Katrina was hoping that this would give her attorney some advantage she was disappointed that Attorney Straits had not appeared and was the one that keep changing the court dates. The only time Katrina saw him was at the little league games and that was not an appropriate place to discuss her civil court case. He was usually dressed in a polo shirt and khaki shorts sitting in the stands. She really believed that having him in the States Attorney's position would help but it backfired. Unfortunately it did not turn out that way. People from his office would show up for the court dates, most of them had just graduated from law school. These individuals really didn't know the case and they were young.

It was October and the next date was schedule for the fifth. The attorney's Santiago, Shoemaker, Weatherspoon, Steward and State Attorney Straits had filed at the counties circuit court a dismissal order and release for a settlement. Katrina was not a lawyer and did not understand the legalities of the state laws. Dean and she had hired attorneys for that purpose. The conditions of the settlement starting from the date and the payments of all sums set forth herein the meaning of Section 104 (a) (2) of the Internal Revenue code of 1986, as amended. The Periodic payments should be to the according schedule spanning 132 months beginning on April 4, 2012 of the amount of $1,500.00 and ending by March 4, 2023. A payment of a large sum of $125, 0000.00 should be given to Mrs. Prue Hallow the mother of Cassandra who is a minor and their attorney Vincent Santiago. The next lump sum payment of $9,623.00 should be given to the payee on April 4, 2023 and on April 4, 2028 another lump sum of $10,000.00. This Settlement Agreement should be construed and interpreted in accordance with all laws of the state. The next part of the settlement was the complete dismissal due to prejudice of all parties and the execution of the settlement. She was utterly bewildered by the outcome. The money would be given in a large sum at first then broken down into payments until the minor Cassandra reached the age of eighteen.

She thought that people by nature were innocent and founded guilty not guilty to be found innocent. Katrina now found it hard to believe in justice within the corrupted court system. Katrina had no idea about court cases except what she saw on television reality series. The settlement and going to the court house was now over, but counseling for all parties had to continue at least until the first of the New Year. The counseling experts then had to report to Judge MacGuire on the continuing progress.

Once Halloween was over it wasn't long before the Christmas holidays were quickly approaching. And fresh falling snow had covered the barren corn and soybean fields. The glistening snow made everything look pure and new again. Just maybe the civil case could finally be closed after two long dreadful years. Katrina did not know that the parole officer along with Judge MacGuire had other plans for the Garrett Family and it did not include Wayne to come home permanently at Christmas. When Christmas Eve came the honorable judge had given Wayne papers and the airlines ticket had been purchased to fly one way to Tucson Arizona to live with the Peabody's', Katrina's parents.

"Dean please tell Wayne to call us once Papa and Nana pick him up from the airport," she was sad about the outcome but now the case was over and maybe she could mend her family back together inch by inch.

"Mom I will and I am sorry about everything," Wayne responded.

"I should be returning from the airport shortly, is there anything you need me to get from the grocery store?" Dean was trying to ease his wives pain as their son was leaving to live somewhere else. He was glad Floyd Peabody had agreed to become guardian. The only thing was Dean still had the financial obligation. He had discussed with Floyd the allowance that would be sent to help take care of Wayne. Wayne would live with his grandparents' and only would be able to come back to see Dean and Katrina once a year with their supervision.

The following year she would continue her counseling and was close to finishing her community college courses to receive her Associate Degree in the Arts majoring in business. Rosa and Junior were adjusting to the new schools. Junior was now a teenager and a freshman in high school. Rosa was starting middle school. Junior was in junior league hockey as an extracurricular program through the small park district. Rosa started to play volleyball for the schools team. This would keep everyone busy during the cold winter months. Katrina enjoyed watching her children at the games. Rosa found she liked playing in the school band and chorus. The year went by quickly.

The 2007 New Year would bring Katrina some more life experiences that she would learn from. Dean was now traveling for his work several times a year. He would travel to Malaysia and stay for a month. He would bring back gifts for Katrina and Rosa. Then he went to parts of Mexico and Brazil. Rosa was working hard to keep hers school grades at a 3.8 G.P.A. Katrina in May graduated with an Associate Degree in the Arts majoring in business and passed the state exam.

Floyd called his daughter on her cell phone after the ceremony. "I am proud of you and your accomplishments."

"Thanks Dad that means everything to me, Oh by the way I received a package today by the postal company. Did you want me to open it?" she was glad that the ceremony was over. Dean, Rosa and Junior had came to the graduation ceremony to see her get her diploma. She had also written a business plans to open a small business in an old farm house. She had started renovating the old farm house the first week of May. She had applied for a small business loan through one of the local banks. She was giving patrons at strip mall samples of fresh international coffees to see what would sell the best at the small shop. She had opened a postal box at a new shipping place and had the papers drawn up for assume name for the company through the state. The new owners of the shipping store was a mother and daughter team. The mother, who was of Spanish descent, was older by ten years to Katrina. She had jet black hair and was always cheerful when she came into the store. Katrina became friends with Ms. Maria Woods. Maria and Katrina both enjoyed specialty teas, coffees and a good book. As the two women became close Katrina would learn that they had more in common.

"Good morning Maria have you read any good novels lately?" Katrina was always looking for one of the best sellers to read.

"Hi Katrina no I have not read any new novels. I would like your opinion about something. I am thinking about putting on these shelves seasonal items to help with sales. I was wandering if I could train you to help me with my shipping store. My daughter that you met at the grand opening lives too far away and I would like some weekends off. My daughter Suzanne agrees that I should find a person trustworthy and close to come to open the store." Maria while talking to her began the task of preparing a box to ship for one of her clients. Suzanne had gone through a divorce several years ago and had custody of Ricardo. She also had a summer home along the lake and a few houses down from Maria. Maria's husband Larry was a retired commercial airlines pilot.

"I don't have a problem helping out Maria but in June I will be working on trying to get the coffee, International teas and bookstore ready for opening day around the fourth of July. I am also in charge of this year's family reunion so I will be having out of town guest." Katrina began helping her friend Maria on a daily basis.

"Katrina I was looking more toward Labor Day weekend for the first time to get away for a few days. Can you check your calendar and let me know. I need to go to the bank sometime this afternoon. Is it possible for you to stay here until I get back?" Maria began getting her items ready to leave.

Katrina kept herself occupied by picking up and taking care of customers at the mailbox and shipping store.

"Go ahead Maria I can stay I was just going to work on gathering information on the Internet for possible companies to order products from." Katrina was finishing put Maria's package ready for the shipping company's truck.

Maria returned quickly and showed her how to use the computer and the different programs for shipping local or International.

"When is Dean gone for his next business trip?" Maria lived close by and was wandering if her new friend would like to come over for cock tails.

"Why do you ask Maria? Dean will leave again in August after the county fair." She replied

"Well my husband, Larry usually goes once a month to a meeting and I thought we could get together for cock tails and a girls evening."

The early summer days were busy for Katrina as she prepared for her opening day and Along with training at Maria's shipping store. Katrina's parents were expected to be here for opening day. Floyd had decided that he would drive the 40 foot RV one last time. In the RV Ruthanne and Wayne found the trip pleasant but long. Floyd was parking the RV at the state park off of route 173 for the next two weeks. They were going to visit Katrina and her family. Then drive up to the north woods to visit their son Frances and his family. Frances, his wife Maggie and their daughter Melinda lived about 6 hours from Katrina's house. Francis, Maggie and Melinda would be down for the family reunion that Katrina was hosting this year.

Once the visiting was done then Floyd, Ruthanne and Wayne would head east to West Virginia and the Appalachian mountains to visit with Ruthanne's extended family. They would stop several times to visit with family and friends. The trip usually took the whole month of July before heading back to the Tucson area. The bookstore was open and the grand opening was a success. Katrina had the local chamber of commerce come and a local paper had interviewed her as a new business owner. The month of July went by quickly. Dean was preparing the building to sell food at the county fair. Katrina at the beginning of August would make the trip into town to give the bank. She had an update of the sales inventory sheet and gives them a list of businesses or nonprofits that had rented the large room. The renting of the room would bring in more profit and balance out the winter months.

When she got to the bank the manager called her into the office. She was hoping that with the documentation from July now the Small Business Loan would go through and she could begin paying off numerous creditors. The bank manager, Crystal Font had the business plan and had been working with her since the end of April.

"Good morning Crystal, I hope you have some good news about the SBL that I applied for has gone through." Katrina said.

"Well Katrina I know how hard you have worked but I have some terrible news. The SBL was denied for your new International Coffee, Tea and Book Store. I am sorry." Crystal replied, then the phone on her desk rang and she answered it. Katrina at first was stunned and got up from the chair. She left the bank and went to her car. Crystal did not explain why the loan was denied and Katrina was a loss of words. However, before leaving the banks parking lot. Katrina sat in the car and began to cry.

"What am I going to do with 100 pounds of green coffee beans?" She looked at her rear view mirror and wiped the tears off. Just maybe Maria can give her some advice and Katrina left to go to the mailing and shipping store.

She arrived at the mailing and shipping store. Maria was busy helping a customer.

"Katrina why don't you go back to the break room and I will join you shortly." She was completing the sale.

Katrina began to shake her head and the tears began again.

"Maria what am I going to do? The bank has denied my SBL and I have this entire inventory to sell. Do you have any suggestions?" Katrina had to get herself together and head over to her little book store.

"I have a suggestion why don't you bring some of the items here and try to sell them. I can also help with moving anything in my 4x4 and Suzanne can help also." Maria was looking over the days sales.

Once Katrina was able to calm down she left for her store. When she arrived at the house that she was renting for the book store she noticed that a new lock was on the door. She was not able to get in and did not understand why a lock was on the door. The SBL was to pay for August rent and she had not been able to pay and now the payment would be late.

She would need to call the land lady and ask her to open the store so she could get all the merchandise out. She would not tell Dean anything until it was necessary. The only thing she could do is go home and get up the next morning to call the landlord Tanya MacFee.

"Good morning is this Tanya MacFee? I am wondering why you put a new lock on the store." Katrina waited for a sensible response.

"You did not pay August rent and you have three days to clear the premises. The items that have been left there will become mine." Tanya was already raising her voice toward Katrina.

"I will give you the money by the 15th of the month." Katrina new now she would have no choice but to close and make the necessary phone calls to return some of the merchandise. She hung up the phone and the next person she called was the book warehouse to see what was needed for the returns. Katrina took some deep breathes and began dialing the number.

"Hello my name is Katrina Garrett I have placed a large book order and now I need to return all of them. Unfortunately I had to close my store do to uncontrollable circumstances."

A young man's voice was on the receiving phone line. "You have reached the warehouse and my name is Arthur. Mame can you please give me the order number and I will look it up on the computer."

Katrina had located the order number. "My order number is K25892 and was placed in May of this year."

"Yes I have found it and it looks like you can return all the books. Please when you return them you will need to have the form filled out and place it each box. Is there anything else I can help you with?" Arthur waited for a reply.

"No that is all I need. I will start sending the books back sometime next week. Thank you Arthur for helping me out and have a good day! Good bye" Katrina hung up the phone. Now she would need to call Maria to see she can help. Maria and I had a barter system to the mailing and returning items. I would work during the holidays at the mailing and shipping store in exchange of mailing out return items. The items that I could not return would be sold at the annual housing development garage sale. She would pay the local people first and then the credit cards. The economy was getting worse for small businesses all over the United States. She had contacted a lawyer that dealt with companies that were going bankrupt but did not want to include the family income. The new bankruptcy laws were stricter compared to the past. When the lawyer went over everything Katrina knew that there had to be other alternatives.

The news media broadcasted that the United States would be in a recession for many years to come. Katrina still had many of the items left from her store and placed them in the basement. The green coffee beans would be placed into large totes and smaller batches would be sealed to lock out any moisture. She opened a store on the Internet and would try to sell items so she could rid of more of the smaller items. The Internet store began to sell and shipping was easy. Customers were buying and Katrina was happy about it. Unfortunately the Internet site would mark up the cost of having a store and added new taxes. Katrina could not believe it; she wandered what else the government would do when it came to having stores on the Internet.

It was late November and the holiday shopping had begun so Katrina started working at Maria's sipping & mailing store. It was still hard for her to accept the fate that was given to her. She would open the store at 9:00 a.m. and be there until 3:00 p.m. when Maria would come in to close.

"Good afternoon Maria, did you get all the errands done that you wanted today?" Katrina had just finished with a customer.

"Yes Thank you and I was able to get some Christmas shopping started," Maria replied.

"Katrina, can you come in on Friday afternoon to help with unboxing a new shipment of items. Then, will you be able to stay to help me set up some new holiday items on the shelves and get ready for a Holiday Sale Special that is coming up?" asked Maria.

"I do not see why not," was her response.

"Have you seen today's news where there was an earthquake of a 7.4 magnitude off the northern and eastern portion of the Caribbean?" Maria was turning on the small television back in the break room to see if there were any updates.

"Oh my, Maria I cannot believe it, no I hadn't heard! Will the United States send any aid to the areas hardest hit?" Katrina was astonished by the breaking news. She was beginning to think that things would only get worse as the world would get ready to celebrate the upcoming New Year.

The nation was collecting items and monetary funds for the earthquake region. Maria had placed a plastic container in the store to collect donations for the relief and for the local pantry.

"Katrina I cannot believe how people are still donating items. Our local economy is the worst in the state and our unemployment is the highest compared to the larger cities. The farm crops were damaged this year due to the unusual weather and prices have gone up." Maria sighed as she put the last of the holiday decorations up.

"I agree Maria and next year is a presidential election. We still have so many of our men and women in the military fighting the war against terrorism. Do you think that we will ever catch Bin Laden?" She stills some anger against the Al-Qaeda terrorist group.

Maria looked up from what she was doing, "I wish we would find the man and have him be tried with war crimes so that the military men and women could come home to their families."

Katrina shook her head to agree with Maria. It was after 8 p.m. and they had accomplished getting everything done.

"Well that will do it!" Maria began to close up the store and started using a knick name for Katrina.

"Hey Kat do you want to go to the square, there is a new pub there. I thought we could get a drink and maybe a bite to eat before going home." Maria turned on the alarm and locked the door with a key.

"Sure that sounds great," Kat replied.

They walked to the pub and it was busy for a Friday night. The pub owners had a disc jockey playing the latest hits. The girls took a corner booth.

"Do you have any plans for New Years Eve?" Maria was looking at the menu. Katrina was looking at the menu also as the waitress stopped at the booth to take their order.

"Maria what are you going to order?" Kat wasn't really hungry so she was looking more at the appetizers.

"I am going to order the seafood appetizer and a Corona." The waitress came over to the booth and her name tag had Terri on it.

"Ladies what can I get you to drink tonight? Are you ready to order?"

"I would like a seafood appetizer along with a Corona," Maria stated.

"And I would like to order your nacho platter with a classic margarita," said Kat.

"I will get the order in right away and bring you your drinks." Terri then walked over to the order window and to the bar.

"Here are your drinks ladies and your water. Is there anything else I can get you tonight? The appetizers will be out shortly." Terri stated.

"About your other question Maria; we currently have no New Years Eve plans." Kat was slowly drinking her margarita.

"Why don't you, Dean and Rosa stop by Suzann's house to celebrate? She will be coming in from the city to help for the holidays and is having a small party. She is going to have music and plenty of food," Said Maria.

"Actually Maria that does sound nice; Rosa needs a change and both of us like to dance. I think Terri is bringing our appetizers, "replied Kat.

"Ladies your appetizers, is there anything else I can get you, "Terri placed the platters in the center of the table along with extra napkins.

"This is great, I would like another Corona," Maria began to eat some of the nacho platter.

"Would you like another classic margarita, "Terri was waiting for Katrina to answer.

"Yes go ahead and bring me another classic and can you bring another glass of water with a slice of lemon," Kat responded.

"Ladies, I will be right back with the drinks," said Terri.

"This is going to be just enough tonight," Kat was munching on the seafood platter.

The D.J. had finished playing for the night and all you could hear was the big screen television sets turned to one of the sporting events.

"Here are your drinks, can I take this away. Is there anything else I can get you the kitchen will be closing? Is this together or on a separate check?" said Terri as she took out the check order.

"No nothing else thanks and it can be on one check if that is okay Kat." Maria took out cash to pay the bill. The extra is for your tip Terri. The food was excellent," Maria stated as she finished of her beer.

Katrina had finished her drink and was putting on her winter coat to go outside. It looked like it was snowing again. Maria put on her winter gear and both of them walked to their cars that were parked in the squares parking lot.

"I am tired of the winter weather. I will talk to you later Kat. Have a good night." Maria got into her Jeep Durango and headed home. Katrina had not left yet because she was giving the car some time to warm up. Then she drove home and went to bed.

The next morning the fresh snow was glistening from the sun hitting it just right. The area had only gotten a few inches and it was just enough to make the roads slushy.

Dean had already left for work. Rosa and Junior were still in bed since they were on winter break from school. Wayne was on Christmas break too but the weather in Tucson was delightful. Katrina envied that part of Wayne's life. Christmas Eve and Christmas day went by quickly. Dean, Rosa and her had left to go to Suzanne's New Year's party around 10:30 pm. When they pulled up music could be heard outside. Katrina knocked on the door. A young man opened the door and told them to come in. It was one of Maria's grandson's that was home from college for the holidays.

"Hi you must be the friends my Nana mentioned. Come on in and you can put your coats upstairs on the couch. I am Maria's grandson Jason," he shut the door behind Rosa.

"Yes I am friends with your Nana. I am Katrina but your grandmother calls me Kat for short, my husband Dean and my daughter Rosa. She is a freshman in high school."

"Everyone is downstairs in the family room and the food is upstairs on the kitchen counter. Just help yourself. The alcohol drinks are down stairs in the bar area and other drinks are in the cooler next to the bar." Jason was heading downstairs toward the music. Rosa followed behind him. Katrina and Dean went to look for Maria. All of Maria's children and a few of the grandchildren were there to celebrate the New Year.

Katrina grabbed a paper plate and put some munches on it and began to carry it downstairs. She saw Rosa and Jason dancing to one of the latest hits. Dean followed her with his own plate filled with food.

"Happy New Year Maria," as Kat put her food down to give her friend a hug.

"Happy New Year Kat and Dean! Are you making any New Year resolutions?" Maria was drinking a cocktail and watching the young adults dance.

"No I do not make any resolutions simply because it is too easy to fail, "stated Kat.

"Hi, Suzanne Happy New Year!" Kat said with an octave higher so she would be heard over the music.

"Happy New Years Kat. Here is a glass to toast with along with a hat. Do you want one for Dean too?" Suzanne was handing here the glass.

"Thanks, but Dean would not want the hat," Said Kat.

Then it was time for everyone in the room to began the count down for the New Year; 10;9;8;7;6;5;4;3;2;1 and Happy New Year 2008 was said in unison. Katrina and Dead gave a kiss at midnight and then danced to one slow song. Then it was time to say our goodbyes before going home for the night. Katrina gave her friends Maria and Suzanne hugs.

"I will call you next week Maria. I am planning to go to one of the stores in the square that is hiring to try to earn some money to pay some of the credit debt from opening my store," said Kat as she left to go to the car where Dean and Rosa were waiting.

New Years Day was spent watching the football games and just chilling. Next week everyone would go back to the routine of their daily life. The days in January and February would seem to drag unless she kept busy working. She had applied at the Family Saver Store and had an interview. She would start her training tomorrow when the store would open. The owner Clayton Willows and his family owned the store. He was at least 6'4" towering over Katrina but had a teddy pair deposition. He always seems to have a smile on his face and this morning he was making up the next several weeks on the schedule. Katrina found working relieved some of the stress and anxiety she had about the finances. Clayton and his family had moved north from the state of Mississippi after losing everything they owned from Hurricane Katrina. The opportunity of owning a store was only a dream at one time for Clayton. Since, the family had to start fresh it would now be a reality for them. He didn't talk much except for why they were living in the Midwest.

One morning when Katrina was scheduled to open the Family Saver Store she was listening to the news while eating breakfast. Everyone had left for school or work except her. The newscaster came on the air at the local station.

He was an anchor person stating, "Breaking news, just in the stock market worldwide to the lowest since 9/11 and it will be noted as Black Monday. The economist predicted that the worst is still to come and that the domino effect would affect everyone."

Katrina sighed and turned off the television station and grabbed her winter coat. She knew things were bad especially in the county they lived in and many of the houses on her street were abandon or in foreclosure.

The January days went by quickly and Valentine's Day was this week. She had contacted the attorney general's office to check on a way to consolidate her payments for the closed business. She was still waiting for a reply and she had started saving some to travel to Mississippi for the family reunion that would be held in July. Dean have scheduled vacation time at the office and had the two weeks set aside in May for Wayne's high school graduation. Katrina was looking forward to seeing her son and family in Arizona. There were times Katrina was saddened by missing Wayne's growing pains through the adolescent years, but as time went by it was easier for her to accept the decision of him living there.

She had missed Wayne getting his driving license, Prom, meeting his friends and visiting colleges or universities. She had just mailed a care package to Wayne for Valentine's Day and he would call her to let her know when he got it she was sure of it. The days went by and Valentine's Day; February 14th was here and Katrina was on a regular basis opening the Family Saver Store. She had found a local radio station to be played in the store as she was placing spring items by first labeling with the price and restocking the shelves.

The radio station was easy listening and she only had a few customers come in to pick up some household cleaning items. Katrina was not anticipating in bad news this week. She had told Dean that she did not want to do anything special since both of them had to work.

The customers that came in usually didn't talk except thank you at the cash register. It was mid day and Clayton had come into the office and break room for a shipment.

"Katrina, why don't you go home early today? There is a winter storm warning out for the area. I will close up tonight early after the shipment arrives," said Clayton.

"Are you sure, I have already emptied the new items, priced them and restocked the shelves," Katrina was glad that it was an early day and was already grabbing her coat.

"Have a good evening," Clayton replied.

Katrina clocked out and left. When she got into her car she turned on the radio. The radio announcer broke in during the music.

"To our entire listener's out there, the state police have been called to the Northern Illinois College campus. There are student's trying to leave because a gun man possibly a student shooting class mates. We will bring you updates as it unfolds. Now back to the music."

Katrina pulled into the garage. Rosa and Junior were busy during their homework when she came home. She would start dinner and put on the five o'clock news. Rosa had come into the dining room to ask for help on a writing assignment for her English class.

"Mom did you hear what happened down at N.I.U.? Also I need some help with trying to think of a thesis statement for this assignment," Rosa was looking at the handout with the choices to write about and had circled the two she was interested in.

"Yes Rosa, I heard the news. I will help you with your homework as soon I get the meatloaf into the oven. Have you picked what topic you are writing about?" Katrina looked over as she put the loaf pan in the oven and set the timer.

Then she washed her hands and turned up the volume of the television as the news came on.

"This is Channel 4 with the update of what happened on the campus of Northern Illinois in Dekalb. The gun man that entered the lecture hall is dead along with approximately 24 causalities; 18 injured, and 6 fatalities including the gunman himself. The reasons are unknown why this man went on a killing spree."

Katrina was astonished by what had happened, so turned off the television and joined Rosa at the dining room table to help her with the homework. This kind of news was becoming normally along with the military actions in the Middle East. The constant attacks by military troops finding Al-Qaeda cells and destroying them. Yet, they still had not found Osama bin Laden.

"Rosa now that you have chosen the topic to write about the first thing you need to do is make an outline. You should try to make complete sentences. Once you have completed it I will look it over and make any corrections that are necessary," she watched her daughter get busy with the task.

Junior had come upstairs to see if dinner was ready.

"Junior, I have a meatloaf in the oven. It will ready in about 20 minutes. I am putting a pan of water on the stove for the egg noodles. Did you finish your homework for tomorrow?" she would need to cut the fresh vegetables up to add to the menu.

"Mom, do you need me to do anything else. I have all my homework done and have read ahead for the midterm scheduled at the end of the week." Junior was pacing looking for something to do.

"Why you help cut up some of the vegetables and place them in a serving bowl. Then set the table and don't set your Dad a place because he is working late tonight," she helped Rosa move to the other room so that the table could be set for dinner.

"Mom, I did what you said to do with the outline," Rosa help up the paper.

"Rosa that looks fine, after dinner I will take a look at it," she had taken out the meatloaf and was slicing it to put it on the plate. Okay everyone comes to the table to eat," she poured a glass a milk and sat down at the end of the table.

Dinner was over then Rosa cleared the dirty dishes from the table and rinsed them off to put them later in the dishwasher. Katrina had sat down on the couch with Rosa's paper in her hand. She began to read and add the corrections on the side. It didn't take long before it was time to go to bed.

The month of March approached like a lion when it came to the weather and was relentless to let spring make a debut. Katrina was tired of winter and was looking forward to the new buds on the flowers and trees. Spring break for Rosa and Junior was next week but the family had not scheduled any vacations during the time; since in two months they would fly to Arizona. They were all looking toward the trip of getting away and seeing Wayne. She had been sending extra money to Wayne to help in purchasing the needed graduation package and to help with the prom. She had received the senior photo package and mailed them out to all the relatives. She had also sent Floyd some money to help with paying for the grad party. The first day of spring had gone by and the weather looked like it might start getting warmer. The Easter holiday was at the end of the month and some of the early spring bulbs were popping up from the soil. April looked like it was going to be a busy month and she was working more hours so she would make the necessary payments for her debt. Clayton had gave her more responsibilities and she was still on some days helping Maria out at the shipping store. Katrina had bought a new dress for the occasion and Rosa was wearing the dress she had worn during the high school home coming last fall. Dean would be traveling for the office to Asia and be gone for most of the month.

She would play single mom once again. Although, she knew that Dean needed to travel more now than ever to maintain stability of keeping employed. She had given Clayton the vacation time.

She was going to work this morning but Clayton had called the night before to ask her to come in early to talk. The spring sun shine was bright in the blue sky. She had seen the kids off to school and was leaving for work. She arrived at the Family Saver Store and Clayton's motorcycle was parked by the door. She used her key and walked back to the office.

"Good morning Clayton, is everything alright?" said Katrina.

"Yes, everything is fine, I called you to come in early to show more managing steps of the store and I also want you to look at these applications. Since, you will be training them as fill INS while you are on vacation with your family," Clayton handed her several applications.

"Do you want me look at them right now? Or later?" she replied.

"I prefer you to look at them now so I can call them and schedule them to come in, if that is alright with you?" Clayton turned on the security camera and looked at the time. Katrina began to read each application. Two of the people were high school students' and one was an older women.

"I think the older women should work the daytime if possible and then have these young women come in after school. Do you want me to call them to set up an appointment to come in?" she handed the applications back to Clayton.

"Thanks that would help me out a lot, my wife has a doctor appointment tomorrow and I have to take her there." Clayton looked at his cell phone to see if there were any new messages. Then he grabbed his motorcycle helmet and put it on.

"Again thanks for everything. I will call later toward closing to see how everything went. If there is any trouble just leave a voicemail on my cell," as he went out the door.

Katrina picked up the office phone to call the two people she felt would help at the store. The first person was an older woman that lived close to the county herb and berry patch farm.

"Good morning is this Matilda Barns? My name is Katrina and I am the manager of the Family Saver Store at the square. You recently filled out one of our applications. I like you to come to the store later this morning for an interview. Is this possible?" this was something she was new at but hopefully the person on the other side of the phone didn't hear the nervousness.

"Good morning yes this is Matilda Barns. I don't have to be at my other job until one o'clock this afternoon. Of course, you think that the interview will last for more than an hour. So can I come by, around 11:30 if this is okay," Matilda responded.

"That sounds fine and I am looking forward to meeting you in a few hours. Good bye Matilda," Katrina hung the phone up to dial the other number for the high schooler. She dialed 865-2149 and the phone on the other end began to ring. A woman picked up the phone.

"Hello, this is the Ashtonn resident's," Mrs. Ashtonn replied.

"Yes, Hello and good morning. I am calling for Sky Ashton in response to a job application that she recently filled out at the Family Saver Store. I know she is in school, so can I leave a message for her," Katrina had glanced at the security camera to see that there was a mother with a young child in the store.

"Of course, let me get a pen and paper to write the message," Katrina could hear Mrs. Ashtonn shuffling things looking for something to take the message. Okay, I am ready so what is the message?" Mrs. Ashtonn replied.

"My name is Katrina Garrett, I am the Family Saver Store manager our store number is 865-2119. I need Sky to call me so I can set up a time for her to come in for an interview. The sooner the better for both of us. Can you please give her the message?" Katrina waited for a response.

"Will that be all, Mrs. Garrett?" Mrs. Ashton stated.

"Yes, thank you and I am sorry but I need to go and take care of a customer," She responded. "Good bye!" Katrina hung up the phone. She hurried out the office door and slightly shutting it as she made her way to the cash register. The young women had her arms full of household cleaning supplies and at the same time trying to keep hold of the little girl. She finished taking care of the customer so that she could get back putting the inventory list into the computer. She was making an ordering list for the upcoming months. She was typing when she noticed a woman come into the Family Saver Store and by the cash register. She finished putting the last item into the Excel program and hit the save button on the computer. The morning had gone by quickly and it was almost time for lunch. The woman that was in the store might be Meltilda. She shut the door to the office and walked over to the register.

"May I help you look for something?" Katrina asked.

"Oh I don't think so I here for an interview with Mrs. Garrett the manager," she replied.

"Yes I'm Mrs. Garrett, the manager," she stated.

"I have good news you are hired and training begins Friday at 3 p.m. sharp, is there any problem with it. Please give me a call as soon as possible. If you have any questions feel free to ask anytime," stated Katrina.

"I don't think so, I work part time as a waitress at the Corner County Restaurant but my hours have been cut again because we don't get enough people in there. This job is to help make up the financial difference," Meltilda responded.

"Okay, then I will see you Friday morning about this time," she commented to herself that the floor would definitely need mopped tonight before she went home. The day seems to drag until after the schools were let out for the day. Then customers like teenagers and people on their way home would stop in to see if they could find an item cheaper and at a discount. Everyone was hurting when it came to finances.

Katrina checked her email and noticed Dean had sent a note along with confirmations for the trip next month and hers in July. The email read.

"Katrina here is the PDF of confirmation from the airlines for the flight in May along with the car and hotel confirmation. The other PDF is airline confirmation for your trip in July. I will be able to Skype tonight around nine o'clock. Talk with you. Love you Dean." Katrina signed out of the email and finished working. Tonight there had been two customers around 5:30 and afterwards there had been no customers. She decided to start mopping the floor and the routine of closing. This way she would actually leave to go home on time. She finished up counting the register, turned off the lights except for security and locked up. She had a little more time tomorrow morning since she wasn't scheduled to come in until 12:30. Clayton was opening and wanted to bring in some boxes he picked up from the warehouse in the city.

She got home to a semi-clean house and Junior had made dinner. The leftovers had been put into the refrigerator. Katrina took out the food and warmed it up in the microwave. She took her plate to the bedroom and signed into her e-mail so she could make a copy of the confirmation PDF and start up Skype. Then she would talk to Dean for an hour or so before calling it a night. Rosa and Junior were both in their rooms finishing up their homework. April rains had made the grass greener, the trees fuller with leaves and daffodils were blooming. The temperatures had been getting warmer and soon the month of May was upon us. May meant the trip was only a few weeks away, Memorial Day and the first sign of summer frenzy. Since she had the morning off tomorrow she would go through her email account, make an appointment for Peter with the groomer, and call the kennel to take Peter while they were gone in May. She also needed to go to the post office to stop the mail. Dean would return home right before Mother's day weekend.

She was ready for bed and had talked to Dean on Skype. So far everything was ready for the trip to Arizona. The next morning she woke up earlier that usually to watch the sun come up over the horizon. She had turned on the teapot so she could have her morning tea. The soft color of red and oranges lit up the sky. It was going to be another beautiful day but possibly some showers later in the day.

She watched her neighbor Billy go to his small shed to get the birdseed for the birdfeeders in his yard. The mornings were quiet until Rosa's alarm went off to get her up for high school. The alarm went off and Katrina began her morning routine. She would drive both Rosa and Junior to school each morning, but they would need to ride the bus home.

She had noticed after taking the children to school that her neighbor had not left for work. This would be the perfect time to ask him to watch the cats. Billy was outside again working on his beautiful flower garden. She parked the Elantra into the garage. She then walked to the back yard of Billy's small ranch style home to talk with Billy.

"Hi Billy, I noticed that you did not go into work today. Is everything okay?" said Katrina.

"Good morning Katrina. No everything is fine. I took today off because later this morning I have to go see the doctor. Since I had some time this morning I thought I would weed the flower beds," he replied.

Katrina watched him pull out the weeds for moment. "Well I hate to bother you, but on May 20th we are flying down to Arizona to see our son Wayne graduate from high school. I was wandering if could watch the house and make sure the cat bowls have water and dry food. You won't need to take care of the dog. I have reserved a spot for Peter at the Kennel," she replied.

Billy was a man in his mid 50's with hair peppered with gray, like most days he worked in his yard. He was dressed in jeans and a t-shirt usual had sayings that depicted the sport of fishing.

"Hi Billy this year's flowers really are blooming for you," Katrina stated.

"Yes, they are really nice this year. I noticed that Dean's Honda was not in the drive way the last couple of days. Is Dean camping with the boys group or away on business again?" Billy replied.

"Dean is on business trip and will be home sometime next week," Katrina answered. I have a favor to ask you. We will be on vacation the Wednesday before Memorial Day. We are flying down to Arizona to see Wayne graduate from high school. Please could you keep an eye on the house and make sure that the cats have fresh water and food each day that we are gone. I am taking Peter on Wednesday morning to the Kennel and I have already done the paper work to stop the mail," said Katrina.

"I don't see why not. When will you be back?" Billy asked while picking up some of his gardening tools.

"The flight leaves Wednesday afternoon on May 22nd at 4:00 p.m. and we return on Tuesday, May 30th at 4:00 p.m. I will pick Peter up on Wednesday morning from the kennel when they open that day. I can bring over a house key tonight and I will write the information down in case you need to reach me." She continued to talk as she was walking next to Billy.

"I will leave a note on the kitchen counter for you along the dry cat food."

"That sounds fine. I will see you later tonight," Billy replied.

Katrina worried about Bill. Since his wife had died several years ago and he was living on his own. The last few months she had noticed that he had a limp in one of his legs. Maybe that was why he was going to the doctor today.

Katrina went back into her house and went to look for her note pad where she kept a check list of things that needed to be done before they left at the end of the month. She jotted a few more things down on the list. She took a quick shower and wrapped a towel around her. She walked to the kitchen to make a sandwich and have a glass of milk. She glanced at the electric version of a grandfather clock to see the time. She had to get moving so she wouldn't be late for work. She took the food back to the bedroom and took a bite of the sandwich. She got a pair of caprice out of the closet along with a polo style shirt. She put on a pair of tennis shoes and took one last bite of her sandwich. She grabbed her purse and keys, took the last swallow of milk and walked to the kitchen to put the glass into the sink. It was off to work for the afternoon.

The days went by quickly and Dean was on his way home. He had told Katrina that he had bought her and Rosa's birthday gift overseas. Katrina was surprised by the thought and began to wander what he had bought her and Rosa. He would be home tonight sometime after dinner.

Katrina was actually looking forward to Dean finally coming home. I had finished cleaning up the kitchen and relaxing in the living room. Rosa and Junior had gotten dressed for bed when the garage door opened. Dean walked through the door. Rosa came running into the room and gave her a big hug.

"Dad what did you get me?" Rosa said.

"Can you wait a moment for Dad to get into the house, before you badger him with questions," she looked at her husband and daughter.

Dean headed toward the bedroom with his suitcase and his briefcase, and then laid them on the bed. Rosa was quickly following him and I came in shortly after.

"Honey this bag is for your birthday. I had a layover in Hong Kong and found a tea shop in the airport terminal."

"Where is Junior?" he put the small t-shirt for his son over to the side. Then took out two shopping bags out of his suitcase.

"Dean, Junior is playing another video game on PS2 before going to bed, you could probably give the t-shirt to him tomorrow," Katrina stated as Rosa tried to be patient.

"Rosa, this bag is yours, I hope it fits," he handed it to Rosa. Rosa looked inside the bag to see a blue skirt and matching jacket, then a smaller bag that had a beautiful necklace.

"Dad, I will try on the skirt right now and I really like the necklace." Rosa took her new treasures in the bag and ran to her bed room. Dean handed her a rectangle box that had a set of four Asia tea cups and a bag of green tea. He then gave her another bag that had a red kimono.

"Dean, the kimono is beautiful and I cannot wait to try the green tea in the morning," Katrina gave Dean a kiss to let him know how she felt.

Rosa came back into their bedroom to show her parents that the skirt fit.

"Mom and Dad look at me," Rosa had a smile on her face.

"Rosa you look like a princess," her mom said.

"Okay, now we need to get our princess into bed. I will help you Rosa hang up the outfit and tuck you into bed. Your Dad has had a long day and he needs to unpack. Then he needs to get some sleep. Say good night to your Dad," Katrina said.

"Your Mom is right and I will see you in the morning," Dean begun unpacking.

Katrina took Rosa into her bedroom. Rosa slipped off the skirt and handed her mom the skirt. Katrina found a hanger and hung it up in the closet. Rosa put on her night gown and got into her bed.

"Okay, sweetie Mommy loves you," Katrina kissed her on the top of her forehead.

Katrina went back to the bedroom where Dean had finished unpacking his suitcase. He was already in bed.

"Babe is everything ready for us to leave in a week for the graduation?" unfortunately, Dean was already asleep and snoring.

Katrina climbed into bed and would ask Dean the question tomorrow.

The next week went by quickly and she was starting to pack the suitcases. They would leave in the morning for the kennel to drop off Peter and head to the airport. This was the first time the family had been back to the Arizona area in six or seven years. Then it had been three-in-a-half years since they had seen Wayne. Dean made reservations at the hotel north of the city so that they could go to the Friday evening graduation ceremony then back to hotel afterwards. My mom and dad had rented the church's kitchen area for the graduation party. She would need to be at her mom and dad's house by 11:30 Saturday morning so that they could follow them to the church to put up the decorations. She had sent a check earlier to her parent's to help pay for some of the catered food. She had sent extra money for the senior package and had some table center pieces sent to her parent's ahead of time.

Today was the day Dean, Rosa, Junior and her had just dropped off Peter at the kennel. The traffic to the international airport was the usual bumper to bumper. She never like the traffic and would try to read a novel or newspaper to occupy herself while Dean drove. The exit was to the right of the off ramp. They would leave the car in a garage and pay the fee at the airport garage. Dean had made online reservations for the airlines and printed out the ticket at home. The most time consuming was not the trip on the airlines per say but the security that everyone had to go through and the carryon luggage had to be a certain size. Then there was the amount of carryon allowed per person while nail clippers, liquids above a certain ounce, food and many other items were no longer allowed on planes because of new regulations and terrorism threats.

They would land at the International Phoenix Airport by 5 p.m. mountain time. They checked in at Gate C and waited in the section to be called. Katrina did not like the airports but it was better than driving.

I had brought a book and a word search to do until the airline staff began calling people to board the plane according to the seating.

"Attention, People that have the seating for A1 through B6 can line up to board. The plane will be on time today." The woman behind the consol was looking at the tickets.

She looked at her ticket and started to get out of the chair. She would be in the next grouping. Dean had the seating for Rosa nest to her while Junior was next to him a few seats behind them. She was starting to feel anxious as they boarded the plane. Taking off was hard for her because she was afraid of heights.

"Rosa, you can sit near the window and I will next to you here." She let Rosa in first and followed. Shortly another woman sat next her on the aisle seat. She herself comfortable and took out her word search.

"This is the captain speaking, I am Caption Edward Standson I will be flying you to Phoenix today where it is currently sun and a warm temperature of 88 degrees. The stewardess will go over the safety flight protocol and then we will taxi on the run way. I will also put on the seat belt sign. Have a nice trip"

The flight was uneventful. She had been reading the romance novel she brought and Rosa was busy looking out the small window at the fluffy white clouds. The stewardess was bringing a drink and snack cart down the narrow aisle. Rosa had brought some reading and homework with her since she would miss a few days of high school.

The stewardess's name tag had Dawn on it.

"Would you like anything to drink?" Dawn asked while she brought out the plastic cups.

"Yes, she would like a Sprite to drink and I would like a Screw Driver to drink," Katrina replied as she handed Dawn a five dollar bill for the alcoholic beverage. She was hoping that it would relax her for the rest of the flight. The stewardess handed them their drinks with a small package of mixed nuts.

She sipped her drink and ate her nuts while reading. Then before long Captain Ed was back announcing that they would be landing in approximately 30 minutes. The seat belt sign was flashing red and the little table had to be back up. The seats had to be brought up and all electronics had to be turned off.

"Please stay seated until we come to a complete stop. Also give the stewardess any garbage that you have. I want to thank you for flying with us today. We are at Phoenix International Airport, the temperature is 94 degrees and sunny," Captain Ed finished the announcement and the air plane now was descending to the air strip.

"Mom, do you think we can go to the hotel first before going over to Nana and Papa's house?" Rosa was gathering her belongings.

"We will see, I think with are going to Nana and Papa's house just to visit and tomorrow we are eating lunch there," Katrina replied.

She and Rosa stood up to wait in line to get off the airplane. She had notice that Dean and Junior had already gotten off. They would be waiting near the exit door in the gate room for them. They would need to hurry to get their luggage from the baggage carousel to head to the car rental area. Dean had late arrival and a minivan reserved for them to use while they were in town. She and the kids would wait outside in the shade while Dean took care of the rental. It did not take him long and he was out the door. He started to walk toward the minivans and clicked on the key. The back lights came on.

"That is the van I rented, it should be unlocked. I will put the big pieces of luggage in the back. Rosa and Katrina sit in the passenger section; Junior you are sitting up front." Dean said as he put the suitcases and directed everything. He climbed into the driver's seat and put the AC on while pulling out unto the major highway. They were heading toward the hotel. She would call her folks now so they wouldn't worry.

"Hi mom, we arrived a little while ago and are heading to the hotel. Is there anything we need to pick up on the way to your house tomorrow?" she asked.

"Why don't you pick up some subs for lunch and I have chips here at the house? I will call you in the morning to let you know the types of subs and what to get on them." Her mom replied.

"Oh, by the way we will be staying at a Holiday Inn Room 227 north of the city," said Katrina.

"Okay I wrote the room number down on the calendar. We will see you tomorrow and then we can talk," Ruthanne responded. She was glad her daughter Katrina had made the trip down for the graduation.

"Dean we will need to be at Mom and Dad's by 11:30 for lunch and we need to pick up subs for lunch," she said then went back to looking out the window.

Dean put the address into the GPS of his smart phone for the hotel. It was about a twenty minute ride to the hotel from the airport. Dean parked the van near the front entrance to the hotel and got out to register at the desk.

"Okay, we are all set. Is anyone hungry? I thought we would just order a pizza for tonight and have it delivered." Dean just wanted to relax before the days to come were going to be busy.

"Dean that sounds good. I am going to go and put my swimsuit on and go to the hot tub. Rosa, do you want to take a quick swim before the pizza arrives?" She got into the suitcase, grab her swimsuit and flip-flops. Rosa did the same. Just come and get us when the pizza is here," she said.

Dean replied, "we'll do!"

Katrina and Rosa left the hotel room. The pool area was nice and there was no one there. She grabbed a couple of towels off the shelve and found a lounge chair to relax in. Rosa went to the deep end of the pool and jumped in. She began swimming the length of the pool. She walked over to the hot tub and turned the switch on for ten minutes and got in. The bubbling and hot water felt good on her lower extremities. Junior came down to the pool area just as the timer for the hot tub turned off.

"Mom and Rosa the pizza is here. I will meet you up in the room," said Junior.

She began to towel dry herself off as Rosa got out of the pool. She handed another towel to her to dry off. As they left the pool area they dropped off their wet towels into the laundry pouch. They headed to their hotel room as she unlocks the door with her security key she could smell the aroma of pepperoni.

"Boy I am hungry. Dad did you get some cheesy bread or breadsticks," Rosa grabbed a hot slice of pizza and sat down at the small round table.

"By the way, did you by chance order my Julian salad?" asked Katrina.

"Yes, with the dressing on the side. It is in the refrigerator," replied Dean.

Junior was watching television and eating his pizza. On the other hand, Dean was in the sitting room of the suite busy on his laptop so he could check various emails from the office. Katrina went into the bathroom to change into bed clothes. Then she headed to the refrigerator to get her salad. She began eating her salad, while everyone finished what they wanted to eat. Junior went into the other room to change into pajamas.

Katrina opened the closet to pull out the roll away bed and made it up for him. Rosa threw her crust from the pizza she ate into the garbage.

"Mom where do I sleep?" Rosa was tired too.

"You are going to sleep in the other full size bed. Rosa did you brush your teeth?" she replied.

"No all I did was floss," Rosa answered as she came from the bathroom ready for bed.

"Ok I guess," she said.

Katrina picked up the room from them eating and climbed into bed. They would have a busy day tomorrow and needed the sleep.

The phone rang and was the front desk ringing their room for a wake-up call. She answered it and slowly got up from the bed. They were to dress in shorts for right now and after lunch get ready for the graduation ceremony.

"Junior, it is time to get up if you are going to take a shower this morning. I laid your clothes out what to wear to Nana and Papa's house," she stated. She quickly folded up the roll-away-bed and scooted it to the side. This way people could get up and start to get ready to leave.

"Mom, I am going into the shower, then I want to go down to the lobby to get some breakfast," Junior grabbed the extra towel and went to shower.

Dean and Rosa were both awake; however, they really did not eat breakfast. Rosa would prefer to eat lunch type foods in the morning. "Honey, I am going to slip on my jogging pants and go down to the lobby to see what they are serving, I will bring up some fresh fruit or bagels for everyone," Katrina responded and finished dressing.

"Okay, while you are gone is there anything that has to be done before we leave to go to your parents'," Dean answered.

"Just put the dress bag and this bag into the car for later," she said.

"Rosa here is your outfit to put on and you need to put the hair brush into the bag in case you need it," she stated and walked toward the elevator. She made it in time for breakfast. There was an area by the entrance that was set up for people to get a continental breakfast. The buffet style had cereal, a juice machine, a milk machine, coffee machine, a fruit bowl, yogurt, a bowl with cream cheese, butter or margarine to choose from, plates, silverware, napkins, pastries, muffins, and then a hot section with hash browns, biscuits and white pepper gravy. She hand two plates; she placed two bananas, an apple, and few pastries on one; then placed biscuits with gravy on the other. Then she went to get a glass and pushed the lever for orange juice. She carried everything up to the room.

Everyone was ready to eat and she changed into more suited attire for the day. Everyone quickly ate and it was time to go. The first stop would be to pick up the sandwiches; Katrina's mom had called while she was downstairs getting breakfast. So, Dean had taken the order for the sandwiches. They were all in the car and heading to Ruthanne and Floyd's house.

They pulled into the drive way. Ruthanne came outside to greet them.

"Hi everyone, did you bring the sandwiches?" Ruthanne asked. Junior and Rosa quickly got out of the car.

"Hi Nana, Junior answered and gave her a hug. "Where is Wayne?" he asked.

"He is waiting for lunch because he needs to eat so he can put on his dress clothes. He has left out the cap and gown so that we can take pictures of him outside in the front yard," responded Nana.

Mom is that the orange tree we got a few years ago for your Christmas gift," Katrina said. She had noticed the tree full of oranges when they pulled into the drive way.

"Yes, it is and we now have to have it trimmed twice a year by a professional. The oranges are so fresh and sweet," she answered.

They walked into the house where Rosa and Junior had said their hellos to Wayne and Papa. Is Martha, Baily and their boys coming over this afternoon?" Katrina asked.

Ruthanne began slicing the long sub sandwiches. "Yes, they will be here any minute. Katrina, can you put the condiments, napkins and plates on the table. This way everyone can serve themselves."

As Katrina finished putting everything on the table. Martha walked into the house with the rest of the family following her. Katrina gave her younger sister a hug.

For a few hours they sat around the dining table eating lunch and trying to catch-up about the events that had happened. Then they discussed the schedule for the rest of the weekend.

"Mom did you a couple of boxes in the mail?" she was hoping everything she ordered as decorations had made it there.

"Yes, I opened one of the boxes to make sure that the order was correct," said Ruthanne.

"That's fine, I will help you clean up the kitchen and then I will go to help Rosa with her hair." Katrina began clearing the table and handed her mom some of the plates that had food leftover on them.

Wayne came in the kitchen ready dressed in his cap and gown.

"You look handsome today and I am proud of your accomplishments," stated Katrina.

Junior came in dressed in navy dress pants and a short sleeve dress shirt. Katrina went onto the spare bedroom and den to check on how Rosa was coming along.

"Rosa is you ready for me to curl your hair with the curling iron," she asked. Rosa had her dress hanging on the back of the closet door.

Katrina began the task of curling Rosa's hair. It took a total of 20 minutes and she was down styling her hair. She went to put her dress on and her make-up. Katrina put on her new dress. The dress was sea foam green and sleeveless. The style of the dress was simple but elegant. She put on her pearl earrings and eye makeup.

"Is everyone about ready? I want to take some snapshots out in front of the house before leaving for the ceremony at the stadium," Stated Floyd. Rosa appeared to be ready. Katrina came out of the room and followed everyone outside.

"Katrina why you stand in front of Wayne and Junior, Dean Stand over here, and Rosa stand on the other side of your mom," Floyd prepared the camera.

"Dad here is my camera it is digital. All you need to do is push this button," she said as she handed the camera to him. Several photos were taken and everyone got into their cars.

They followed the major highway to the stadium where the graduation ceremony was to take place.

"Mom and Dad, I have to be dropped off a door G on the south side of the stadium. Then after wards I will meet you here at door G. I have a surprise for you I also received this to wear over my gown," stated Wayne.

He pulled out the medallion. "I received it for keeping a high grade point average for more than two years. I made the high school's honor society," Wayne responded.

"Your mom and I are very proud of you Wayne. You have need to everyone that to keep faith and hope anything can be accomplished with some hard work," Dean shook Wayne's hand.

Katrina gave her son a hug and she could tell that this was going to be an emotional day. They arrive by door G and she could feel that her eyes were already wet with the hint of tears.

The Golden Sands High School student's graduation was being held at the Snakes Stadium. The Class of 2008 had a total of 1, 020 students graduating and the high school auditorium was too small for the ceremony. Dean found a parking spot and pulled in beside Floyds Jeep Wrangler. They all walked to the entrance and were met by other parents or relatives that had come to see their student graduate. When we entered the double doors several under classmen were handing out a pamphlet that had all the graduating students, guest speakers, valedictorian of the class, and principal. They found enough seats and sat down. Junior sat by Papa in the last seat by the aisle.

The graduation ceremony was proceeding quickly and after the last student received their diploma. The students through their caps into the air and shouted "We Did It!"

The audience stood up and all clapped. The student's began to leave the auditorium out of the side door so they could find their relatives or parents. Katrina was trying to hide the joy she was feeling but the tears started to come after all.

"Dean did you bring a hankie? I really need it to dry my eye," was all she could say. She noticed that even Dean's eyes were a little misty. He was proud of their oldest son on his accomplishments. The auditorium had quickly emptied and now they could go look for Wayne by door G.

"I am going to the ladies room first to freshen up. Rosa do you need to come with us?" Katrina stated as she calmed down.

"Okay Mom. I am coming," replied Rosa.

Floyd, Dean and Junior waited patiently for them in the hallway.

It was only a few minutes when all three of the women came out of the ladies room. They began to walk out the entrance way and Wayne was waiting there for them.

"Hi everyone, what took you guys so long?" he asked quizzically.

"We had to wait for Nana, Mom and Rosa get done in the ladies room," he replied to his brother.

"Dean and Junior why don't you stand next to Wayne so we can take a few more photos. Then we will head back to the house to change into shorts and eat dinner," Ruthanne handed the camera to Floyd.

"You take better pictures than I do," she stated.

Floyd took a few more photos and then they got into their own vehicles. The traffic had picked up since it was during rush hour but they were home in 45 minutes. Everyone entered the ranch stucco style home and changed into their clothes. Everyone ate a light dinner and called it an early night so they could get an early start in the morning.

Morning was cooler to work in and the Arizona temperature was to be in the upper nineties by 3:00 p.m. and the graduation party would be in full swing. Katrina was anxious to meet the girl her son fancied and took to the senior prom along with meeting some of his friends. Floyd's younger sister and her grandchild had driven over from the Albuquerque New Mexico area to be part of the celebration. The table favors she ordered were a big success.

The afternoon went quickly and it was time to clean up the churches fellowship hall. It took everyone to pitch in so that they could finish in one hour.

Once the clean up was done everyone went back to Floyd and Ruthanne's house.

"Junior would you like to stay the night here with Wayne? That is if it is alright with Nana and Papa." Katrina looked over to her parents.

"It is alright with us. Then tomorrow we will meet you for lunch at your sister Martha's house. Or do you want to follow us up?" said Ruthanne.

"Mom, we will follow you up to their house. Although we do have a GPS in the rental car. I would like Dean not to use." She replied.

"Junior would you like to ride up to your aunt's house with Nana and Papa?"

"Yes mom I would, if that is okay," Junior replied.

"Then we will see you tomorrow, Junior you behave and listen to your grandparents," said Katrina. They said their good-byes and went out the door to the van.

Dean drove her and Rosa back to the hotel.

"Mom can I go swimming when we get to the hotel?" Rosa was still wide awake.

"I think we should all take a swim and relax," she replied.

Dean pulled into a hotel parking spot. She knew tomorrow was going to another busy day. The trip to see their son was almost over and she was not looking forward to going home.

"Good evening can I help you sir?" the young man behind the front desk was taking reservations. His tag on his shirt read Cal.

"Yes, I need to have a wakeup call for room 334 at 8am," Dean replied.

"Okay I will put it into our computer," answered Cal.

"Thank you and have a good night," replied Dean. Then he walked over to the elevator to go up to the hotel room.

"Rosa it is time to dry off and go up to the room," said Katrina.

"Okay Mom!" Rosa stated as she climbed out of the pool and then into the hot tub.

"Mom after I am done here in about ten minutes, I will meet you in the room," said Rosa. She relaxed into the bubbling jets.

"Okay I will see you up in the room," she said as she through the towel into the laundry basket near the door. Katrina waited for the elevator and before long the bell dinged for the doors to open. Katrina went in and pushed the button number 3. The doors closed and the elevator went up.

Katrina took out her key card to swipe the door of the room.

Dean was at the table in the corner with his lap top hooked to the hotel's WiFi.

"Hi babe, did you take care of tomorrows wakeup call?" she waited for a reply.

Dean turned to look at her.

"Yes it is for 8 am," he replied and then went back to the lap top.

Katrina headed to the bathroom to take off her swim suit and take a quick shower. She finished and grabbed a towel to wrap around her body. As she came out of the bathroom. She noticed that Rosa was in the room waiting for the bathroom.

Dean had closed the lap top and had a pair of shorts on lounging in the bed. He was busy flipping through the channels to see if by chance there would be anything interesting to watch until everyone went to sleep.

Katrina found her night shirt and slipped it over her head. She laid out her clothes for the next day and climbed into the bed next to Dean.

"Is there anything you want to watch tonight?" He did not see anything so the channel was flipped to the local weather.

"This is fine, because I just want to go to sleep," she replied and turned onto her stomach. She pulled up the sheet just too lightly cover her head.

"Just remember that the only I can sleep is if there is some background noise like the weather or soft rock music," she said as she turned to give a quick kiss tonight.

The Katrina began the routine with the sheet again and got herself comfortable. Rosa took a quick shower and put her t-shirt night shirt on. She climbed into the other queen size bed and took out one of the books she had brought with her on the trip.

Katrina heard something but couldn't determine exactly what it was at first. She slowly opened her eyes and there it was again, it was the room phone. She tapped Dean on the shoulder to answer the phone. He rolled over and picked up the receiver to listen to the recording it was 8 am their wakeup call. Katrina sat up in bed and looked on the night stand for her glasses. She found them and got out of bed. She went to the bathroom and grabbed the jogging pants that were lying on the floor.

She slipped them on and her sandals.

"Dean I am heading down stairs to see what kind of food that the complimentary continental breakfast had available." Her stomach was already growling and knew she needed something to eat. She left the room and decided to take the stairs and quickly go outside for a quick cigarette. She then went into the room where the food was set up on long tables for people that wanted breakfast. She picked up a banana, yogurt, an apple, and some type of sweet roll. She put everything on a plate and went to get a plastic glass to get some juice. Her hands were full and then headed to the elevator so she could go back up to the room.

If they wanted something else Rosa and Dean would have to go back down to get what they wanted for breakfast. The elevator stopped and she walked to the room and tapped the door with her foot. Dean opened the door as Katrina walked toward the corner table. She sat the plate of food down.

"If you guys want something else then you need to get down there before they pick up everything off the tables at 9:30," She sat down on the edge of the bed.

"Rosa you need to eat something this morning," said Katrina. Rosa was fixing her hair in front of the large mirror over the sink and some make-up.

"Mom was there anything there that I will eat? You know how I dislike breakfast foods," said Rosa while she put things away inside her small bag.

"I saw that there were biscuits and pepper gravy that you may like," she replied.

Rosa finished picking up, took the room key on the stand and headed out of the room to go downstairs.

"I am going to take a quick shower and get dressed. I should be ready shortly to leave for Mom and Dad's. Do you think that the skirt outfit is okay for today's luncheon at my sister's Martha's house?" she was putting her makeup bag next to the area by the sink. She was waiting for Dean to say something but again he was on his laptop looking at the various emails he had received on the trip. He was always on call or out of the country for work these days.

"Dean did you hear what I said at all?" she stopped to look at him.

He finally shut down the laptop and put it in his duffle case and looked at her. "I am sorry but a computer on the factory floor crashed and I was emailing to the group that was there how to take care of it. I am sure that the skirt you wear will look fine. You always look nice to me," Dean smiled then winked at her.

"Oh Dean don't start trying to make amends. Were you able to get everything done then? I will repack everything tonight before going to bed. Since, our flight leaves from the airport to Chicago at 3:00 p.m. central daylight hour. I will ask Rosa and Junior to get their stuff together and have any homework assignments finished. I know when we get home we will be tired and just want to relax. I will be picking up Peter on Tuesday before noon," she replied. She then went to take her shower. It was the only private time she still seemed to have. However, sometimes she wishes she had a place that she could escaped to for just a few hours to think and be she.

Katrina had dressed in her light blue denim skirt with a blouse and was putting on some mascara when Rosa walked into the hotel room. Dean glances at the cell phone clock.

"Okay girls we need to go if we want to get to your Mom and Dad's house. I am not sure how the traffic is but I don't want to be late," stated Dean.

"I am ready", she quickly picked up her purse and followed Dean and Rosa to the elevator. They rode the elevator down in silence.

This was the first time they were visiting Martha and Bailey's new house in the north suburbs' of Deer Valley. She was happy to see her sister and her family. Dean pulled the van into Floyd and Ruthanne's driveway. Floyd was waiting for them to get there and was a little annoyed about the lateness that Katrina's family had today. Floyd backed out and Dean followed him to get onto highway 101 north.

The way Dean understood the directions that Floyd had gave him was they would take highway 101 north for about 20 miles then get off and go west for another 10 miles where new houses were being built in a subdivision. The area was just starting to build up of local chain stores in strip malls. The dessert scenery was becoming apparent as they drove further north and now west. They could see where a previous brush fire had taken what plant life but several small shacks like homes that stood on the side of the road empty and ghostly.

They got off the highway and were in a housing development where large family size home was taking on the landscape. They pulled into a drive-way of a stucco two story house.

We excited the vehicles Rosa was at the door ringing the door bell. Inside she could hear someone yell.

"Come in, we are in the kitchen area," her sister replied.

Martha and brother-in-law were busy cutting fresh vegetables for a tray. "Hi everyone just make you at home. Junior the boys are upstairs in the game room. You can go up to see them. Rosa could you put these napkins out on the table for me," said Martha. Rosa took the cloth napkins and set them in a design on the table where the rest of the food would eventually end up.

"Bailey why don't you start barbequing the ribs on the grill and I will finish up in here," said Martha. Katrina looked around her sister's stylish home.

The formal dining area was set up as a buffet with plenty of delicious food. Then on a smaller table were a small cake and other desserts. I took a small dessert plate and put a small amount of mints and nuts on it.

"Martha the food looks scrumptious, but you did not have to put so much work into it," she stated as she put another butter mint into her mouth.

The afternoon went by quickly as everyone got their food and visited with one another.

"Boys did you get some vegs to eat?" Martha looked at her sons plates.

"Yes mom I had a few carrot sticks and cut cauliflower," they answered in unison.

Katrina looked at the time and soon they would need to leave to go back to the hotel. She needed to repack the suitcases so they could get to the airport in plenty of time to drop off the van.

"Junior and Rosa you need to say your good-byes to everyone! We need to get back to the hotel so we can get ready for tomorrow," she said.

"Martha and Bailey thanks again for everything the food was delicious. Mom I will call you once we land at the Chicago O'Hare International Airport." She gave everyone a hug. Dean was already in the van along with Junior. Rosa gave her aunt one last hug and went out to the van. She was last and she hated saying good-bye to her son Wayne. Wayne in the fall would receive a full scholarship to Arizona State University. The next morning after everyone ate from the hotel's complimentary breakfast and loaded the van it was time to go home. Katrina found that taking off was the hardest part of the flight. Dean had taken the van to the return rental section and they were waiting for the trolley to take them to the airport terminal. They checked their baggage and waited for their flight number to be called by the stewardess.

"Flight 378 to Chicago O'Hare will be loading in 15 minutes and we will call seats 1A to 5B first," the stewardess announced over the loud speaker.

The stewardess began calling the next set of numbers. Katrina, Rosa, Junior and Dean were in the next group to enter the plane. They found their seats and the last section of seating was boarding. The flight was on time. The stewardess began the protocol of safety instructions and then the captain came over the speaker. The plane began taxing the runway to take off toward the east. The flight was just over two-in-a half hours, but to Katrina it seemed like it was more than that.

"This is Captain Ryan Cashew today there is thunderstorms in the Kansas area so we will be going north to go around them. There may be some turbulence so please stay in your seat and keep your seat belts on. Again thank you for flying with us." Then the loud speaker went off and the stewardess finished bringing the small drink cart down the narrow aisle.

"Mame would you like anything to drink?" She handed her a small napkin and a bag of pretzels.

"Yes I would like a sprite, something to calm my nervous stomach," Katrina responded to the stewardess. Rosa had woken up from her nap and was looking out of the small airplanes window. Katrina took a quick look to see the thunderhead clouds below and quickly went back to reading. She had problems with height to begin with and looking out the window only made her stomach queasier. Rosa had eaten her pretzels and Katrina gave Rosa her pretzels also.

The airplane took a quick turn and then climbed in the air above the clouds. The stewardess had put the cart away and was buckled in her seat. The plan rocked a little at first but before long the plane seemed fine once again and on the other side a stream of sun was coming through the window where the blind was still up.

The loud speaker came back on and the stewardess had gotten up to walk along the aisle. "This is Captain Ryan Cashew we have cleared the storm and will land at O'Hare airport 10 minutes late but maybe we can make up the time. The weather in the Chicago area is 55 degrees and partly cloudy." The loud speaker was off again.

The stewardess had collected all the garbage from the passengers and was at her station. Katrina went back to reading the magazine. Usually she was not able to cat nap on the flights and today was no different. She didn't understand how Rosa could actually sleep on the plane especially with the type of seats they now had. They were so uncomfortable to even sit in for any length of time. Katrina tapped her daughters shoulder to wake her up and get prepared for the airplane to land at the terminal.

Katrina had told the high school that her children would not be attending school on Wednesday but would be there on Thursday. Rosa and Junior had finished all their absent work for classes. Katrina knew that with them getting in late that tomorrow would be the day to unpack and laundry. She would need to go to the kennel to pick up Peter the next morning and to the post office to get the mail. She was tired and when the air plane finally parked at the terminal she was ready to go home. Dean and Junior were standing up as the stewardess helped passengers to leave the air plane.

"I will meet you in the baggage claims," Katrina said to Dean as he left the airlines.

Rosa and Katrina stood up to reach for their carrying bag that was in the storage compartment above them. It was Rosa's school bag. Katrina put her carrying bag on her shoulder and was in the aisle. Rosa was following now and began to walk briskly to the door.

"Rosa we are to meet Junior and Dad in the baggage area," she said as they got onto the escalator to the baggage claim area. They were to go to baggage claim number 4B and as they got there, the suitcases were on the turn table. Dean was waving his arm above his head to let Katrina know where they were. Katrina and Rosa finally caught up with them and waited for the suitcases. People that were on the flight were taking their suitcases and leaving quickly. Finally, she saw one on their bags. Katrina had tied a piece of colored yarn on the handles to easy mark them so it was easy to spot them on the turn table.

Junior grabbed his bag. Dean's was coming around and he grabbed his and Rosa's. Katrina saw hers and grabbed the wheeled suitcase. They gathered their belongings and went toward the elevator to the parking garage. Dean took out of his pocket the stub and they walked to the vehicle. Dean put all their belongings into the trunk and everyone got into the car. Now it was going to take two or more hours to get home. Illinois toll ways seemed to be under construction again causing traffic problems.

Unfortunately by the time everyone got back into the routine. Dean would leave to go to El Paso, Texas for work at the end of the week for work. Unfortunately she would need to get his laundry done first. The week went by quickly and Sunday morning Dean had already left for the O'Hare airport. The next week was Rosa and Junior's last week of school. The summer days would be here along with the hot and humid weather. Katrina and Dean had opened the pool before he left and Katrina was already planning a pool party. Of course things could change and they would in the next few days.

Peter was acting strange when they got him home from the kennel. She did not think it was anything to worry about but would keep an eye on him anyway. Junior and his best friend Xavier were playing an online computer game and Peter was laying downstairs on the cool concrete floor by the laundry room. She was just going downstairs to check on the last load of clothes and she noticed that the dog was shaking uncontrollably. Katrina kneeled by Peter to calm him, but it wasn't helping.

"Junior and Xavier can you come here for a minute, Peter is shaking and I am going to have to call the vet." She said with a scared tone in her voice.

Junior and Xavier kneeled by the dog, Peter. Katrina went upstairs to call their vet even though she knew that it was after hours. The answering machine had an emergency number to contact and she wrote the number down on a piece of scrap paper.

She dialed the number. "Good evening I have a dog that is a beagle mix and weighs about 40 pounds. He has been in the last shaking uncontrollably and I cannot seem to get him to stand up on his feet. I am not sure what to do at this time." she said.

"Mame you can bring him to the 24 hour emergency vet here on Hickory Ave off of Mulford. We can have our vet look at him."

"Thank you we will be there in about 30 minutes or so," she replied

Katrina went back downstairs were Junior and Xavier were sitting. Rosa had brought down a towel to put under Peter's head. Katrina noticed that the dog's mouth was slightly a jarred but his tongue could not be seen. Katrina opened the dog's mouth to notice that he had swallowed the tongue. She pulled it out and tried to get the dog again to stand. When it did not work she looked around the basement.

"Junior go get two broom sticks and we will need to make a carrier to put the dog on so we can put into the car. Rosa go and get those two old blankets we use to put on the ground for picnics and baseball games." She said as she began the task of making the old style gurnee. Then Junior and Xavier helped put Peter the dog on it. It took all of them to left it and put it into the car. The nurse was waiting for them at the door. She held it open as they all went into a small room.

"I am sorry to tell you that it looks like your dog Peter might have had a seizure. The only thing we can do for him right now is to inject this to help him sleep and never wake up." the nurse said in a calm voice.

Katrina looked at the family dog and was trying not to cry. "Junior and Rosa say your good-byes I will be out in a few minutes," she said in a muffled voice.

Rosa and Junior silently gave Peter a hug, and then left the room. Katrina was petting and caressing Peter's black nose. She knew that the human thing to do what was right.

"Nurse, okay go ahead and give him the shot." She said in a quiet voice. Katrina watched their family dog go to sleep and then she got up to leave the room. She had some papers to fill out and requested Peter to be cremated. She would pick up the ashes before she left for the July 4th Family Reunion. Katrina was sad and was trying to not cry on the way home.

Rosa still had tears in her eyes, "Mom why did Peter get sick?" Rosa was still not sure about that night's event.

"Rosa I don't know. All we know is that Peter might have had a heart attack or a seizure and I am not sure I want to know. I just know he is in a better place. Maybe one day we will get another dog or pet," she said as they turned into the drive way. Now she would need to call Wayne and tell him what happened to Peter. Rosa went to her room and she found her daughter had cried herself to sleep. Dean was video conferencing her in the morning and she would tell him what happened to Peter. She finally went to sleep in an empty bed. The next morning the sun was shining but there was a cool crispness in the air.

Katrina went to the desk and moved the mouse for the desk top computer. She was waiting then the screen dinged to let her know that the conference call was on.

"Hi Dean how was your flight? I have something sad to tell you. Last night I had to rush the dog to the vet. Apparently he had a seizure or something and I had to put him to sleep." Katrina sounded monotone as she spoke.

"My flight was fine Babe. I am sorry that you had to go through that decision by yourself. How is everyone doing?"

"We are making it through. Is you scheduled flight still the same?" she responded. Rosa came into the room to say that she was leaving for her last day of class. It also meant that Junior was waiting in the car for her.

"Bye mom, we will see you around lunch time. Is it alright that my friend Tess comes over to swim later this afternoon?" Rosa waited for a reply.

"I guess that is alright. I will see you later then. Drive safely," she replied. Katrina heard the garage door close.

"I have really nothing else to say. Just try to have a nice day at work and I will talk to you in a couple of days," Katrina wanted to go and get busy with her morning routine. She still had a few things to do before they all left in two weeks on separate vacations.

"Bye, I will talk to you later this week. I should know then if there are any changes. As of right now it looks like I will be home late Friday night," then hung up the call.

Katrina started the outside work first because the weather report was calling for warmer temperatures close to the 100 degree mark. There was a heat advisory out and she really needed to get her mind off of Peter. She was planting red geraniums in the iron wrought planters for the front of the house. Then she would head inside to the air conditioning for the rest of the day.

She went back to the routine and before long it was the end of the week. Dean had messaged her to give her his flight information to come home. Dean was arriving late Friday night after everyone was in bed. She was hoping that he would not wake them up. It was hard for to go back to sleep once she was woken up.

Saturday morning had arrived and she woke up as the sun was rising on the east side of the house. She had left the air conditioning on because it was going to be another hot and humid day. Dean was still asleep along with Rosa and Junior. One of the calico cats had gotten her up for their breakfast. The calico cat Pansy was always waking her up to get her food and open one of the blinds for the morning sun.

The next week went quickly with routine chores and swimming in the evening after dean came home from his commute to the office. This weekend Junior would have Xavier and his other friend Riccardo to stay over for the weekend to celebrate his birthday with a pool party ice cream and bomb fire in the backyard fire pit. They stayed downstairs most of the time staying up all night playing computer or gaming. They would come up to eat and then go back to their gaming. On Monday afternoon Xavier and Riccardo would go home. The party was over and the next week went slow, but Katrina had already begun the task of repacking.

On Thursday, Dean, Rosa, and Junior would pack for a week to go on their outdoor adventure of canoeing and tent camping in the north woods of Minnesota. Katrina had gone to the Post Office to stop the mail the day she left and would pick it up when she returned.

"Katrina did you take of someone to watch the cats and house while we are gone?" Dean asked as he started putting his gear into the trunk of the Civic. Junior had brought up his gear and was waiting by the car.

"Of course, along with stopping the mail. Tomorrow I am driving to the bus service to park my car and ride the bus to the airport. My flight leaves at 1:30 so I will leave a message on your cell phone to let you know I arrived." was her reply.

"Dean did you remember the medical forms, medical cards and Junior's prescriptions? She waited as Dean checked a back pack.

"Yes, they are here in a water proof bag." He replied.

She went back into the house to see how Rosa was doing with her packing.

"Rosa, do you have your packing list?"

"Mom it is right here. I think I have all the personal hygiene products," Rosa looked at her bag and picked it up. "Is Dad packing the car I now we need to get on the road because the trip to where we are going is about nine hours from here." Rosa went down the stairs to the garage and she followed.

"Dad, I am all packed. Here!" Rosa handed her Dad the bag. Junior was already in the passenger front seat. Rosa got into the back seat Katrina handed her a small cooler that had bottle water, pop, fresh carrots and celery in baggies, hard candy and snack foods.

"Thanks Mom!" Rosa said she had placed a pillow against the other door along with a blanket.

She shut the door. A bang was heard while Dean shut the trunk.

"Okay babe we have everything and need to get on the road," Dean gave her a kiss good bye. Then got into the driver's seat, shut the door and pulled out of the drive way. She waved as the car disappeared down the road. Katrina went back into the garage as she entered the house she shut the garage door. Tonight she would finish her packing except for the personal essentials needed to get ready in the morning.

She would eat a quiet dinner and watch some television before calling it a night. She needed to get a good night of sleep before leaving tomorrow since she would be at the airport two hours before her flight. This was a necessity since the devastation of 9/11. The TSA screened everything and everyone entering the International O'Hare Airport. She was able to watch the news and then go to bed. She printed her internet ticket for the bus along with her ticket for the airlines and placed it into her laptop bag.

She arrived at the bus depot and parked her car. She had done the rest of the reservations on her own so she could stay a few days longer to see what the rebuild from Hurricane Katrina. It had been three years and she was hoping that the Mississippi cost had recovered from the devastation. She sat in front of the bus depot on a bench until the bus arrived.

A loud speaker came on and a woman said, "bus for the O'Hare Airport arriving please have you luggage and ticket for the bus driver ready."

The bus pulled up in front of her. She had everything ready and had a book and magazines with her to read. The bus trip was over two hours because of construction on the Illinois toll ways. She stood up and went to the bus door.

"Good afternoon, what airlines are you taking today Miss?" the bus driver took her one suitcase and placed it in the compartment under the bus.

"Sir I am taking the American airlines so I will need to be dropped off at their entrance," Katrina replied. She handed the ticket to him and climbed the bus stairs. There were several other people getting on the bus for their flights. However, the bus seat next to her was empty when they pulled away from the depot. The bus would stop at two hotels to pick up any passengers then they would get onto the toll way to go to the airport. The traffic was not too bad but when she looked up out the window from reading she saw that they were arriving at the airport. Katrina always had a little bit of anxiety before getting onto a airplane but once she was settled into her seat she would chew a piece of gum. Then she would look at a magazine or book while the pilot went over the safety procedures. Then they would taxi to the run way. The airplane had all the seats full and that would mean someone would be next to her.

She had decided to check one suitcase at the curb and have a quick cigarette before going through the necessary check points for security.

It was time to get into the security line. She had her state Id and her ticket out to show the TSA person at the line, and then she took off her shoes. She had learned not to carry much on board because of the hassle of the security. She placed her small purse and shoes into the tote. Then in the next tote she took out her lap top and its bag, and then both totes went on the conveyer belt to be scanned. She walked through the body security scan and on the other side picked up her things. She headed quickly to the gate. She saw a snack bar and picked up cold lemonade to drink while waiting. The American Airlines gate was on the other side of the terminal. She slowed down to read the monitors that had flight departures to see if the flight AA 225 was still on time. She saw that it was and continued to the terminal Gate G. The gate area was already filling up so she found a seat in the corner by the window. She watched people go in and out of the area. She noticed that some were businessmen; there were some college students with back packs, several women of different races traveling by themselves, older couples traveling maybe for a vacation, and only one mother with an infant.

The only reason she knew this was that while taking off the baby or infant begun to cry. She was hoping that the mother would give it a drink or a pacifier to quiet her down. The baby's ears were probably popping because of the altitude. It seemed forever that the infant was screaming, but finally it was quiet in the cabin. A woman sat on the right side of her next to the window.

"Ladies and Gentleman, I am your captain today as we fly to the Biloxi Airport. My name is Captain Jacob St. Peterson and my co-pilot name is Max Strum. We hope that you will enjoy your flight today on the American Airlines. Shortly one of the stewardesses will bring a cart with drinks and snacks. Thank you for flying with us today," Captain Jacob out.

Katrina pushed down the lever to make the seat go slightly backwards and then she pulled out a notebook to jot some questions down to ask her great and uncle when she arrived in Gulfport, Mississippi.

This is Captain Jacob, "Ladies and Gentlemen we will be landing shortly. The weather in Mississippi is sunny and the temperature currently is 85°. We thank you again for flying with us and enjoy your stay."

Katrina could tell that the airplane was descending and had landed on the run way.

"Please stay in your seat until the plane comes to complete stop. Also do not forget to get all of your personal belongings," the stewardess stated and then smiled. The plane parked at the gate and came to a complete stop. Passengers in front of her stood up to get their carryons in the above compartments. She waited patiently as people begun to go pass her to leave. Katrina slowly stood up and went into the aisle of the plane and walked to the door. She would go down to the baggage claim to collect her luggage, and then head over to the rental car booth. She had rented an economy car for the next few days.

The turntable in the baggage claim area was filling up with all colors, sizes and shapes of luggage. Katrina saw the orange pom pom on the handle of her suitcase. She grabbed it as it went by and begun wheeling it to Carmax Rental Center.

There was a young man behind the counter with a name tag of Earl.

"Good afternoon sir, I believe I have a car reserved for the next five days," said Katrina.

"May I have some identification please and the print out of your receipt," Earl took her paper work and begun to type in the information into the computer.

"Here it is Miss, I have everything I need and all I need you to do is sign the paper. I can give you the keys and you can go out this door to go to the car," Earl stated. He handed her the keys and she walked out the door to a row of cars. She had a blue Mazda four door. She opened the trunk and placed her one suitcase inside. She left the car garage to head west toward Gulfport. She could see that several of the casinos had been rebuilt since Hurricane Katrina. The road she had to take was the scenic route along the Gulf of Mexico. The drive was slow because of road construction along the way. She could hardly wait to see everyone tonight in the common area of the hotel. The beaches still look barren especially since it was July and no one was using them. There were houses still partially on the foundations, steps with flowers but no house, and fences around concrete slabs. She was shocked as she entered the city of Gulfport. The area by the Gulf was still in shambles from three years ago when Hurricane Katrina hit at the end of August. There were pieces of houses still in the trees that looked like skeletons. She had notices some remnants of houses boarded up and a number next to the door circled. This to her seemed odd it would be something she would need to ask one of the locals.

She was heading to Diamond Point Hotel by the highway. She found a parking spot and went into the hotel to register. The manager was busy on the phone and computer with hotel guests. She was waiting for him to finish and when he turned toward her, he made a hand jester showing that he would be a few minutes.

She took a seat and looked around the busy foyer. She decided to go and look by the door at the tourist flyers to see what else there was to do in the area. She would be there an extra two days after the family would depart from the reunion.

She looks up to see if the manager was available to check her into her room. She went to the front desk and watched the middle age man file some papers before returning to her. While she watched she could see that this man was probably in his late thirties and stood about five eight in height. He was average built with dark brown hair, a happy go lucky attitude and seemed like he was always smiling at the guest that came into the lobby.

"Hello can I help you?" he stated.

"Yes, I have a reservation and I am here for the Peabody Family Reunion. I believe that my dad, Floyd is already here along with other relatives. They have blocked some of the rooms here for us. But my request was to be on the third or fourth floor."

"Yes mame. I have you on the third floor in room 318. Your family is on the first and second floor. I think some of them are in the back conference room together. They have the room tonight and then tomorrow for the reunion from one o'clock in the afternoon to six this evening. I am the day manager and my name is Toby Jarman. If there is anything you need just ask me."

Katrina smiled, "Thank you Toby I might just do that. May I ask you why did I see some National Guard personal here?"

"Yes of course, they are here to rebuild the roads and the Gulf shoreline from the hurricane three years ago."

"I am here today until nine o'clock tonight and I will be back here tomorrow morning around ten."

"Mame this here is your room card key"

"Thank you and I am sure that I will be fine," she took her card key and went to the elevator. She would go to her room and freshen up before seeing what everyone else was doing the rest of the night.

She put on a summer dress then went out of the room to the elevator. The elevator door opened and she went in push the close button also the lobby button. The elevator door opened into the lobby and she turned left toward the conference room. The door was propped open and she saw her dad Floyd sitting at one of the tables with one of his sisters. This was the only time she was able to see her relatives. She noticed that several of the had made it in for the occasion.

"Hi; when did you and Mom get in today?"

"We got in around noon. Your mom went up to the first floor to see your Aunt Lynette. She is in room 132 with your Aunt Sasha. They are sharing the room to save on expenses. Also your Aunt Lynette might need some help," he replied.

"Well I will go up to see Aunt Lynette and Aunt Sasha to see if they need anything. What are you doing for dinner tonight?"

Just as Katrina was to leave her Aunt Blanche walked into the room with three large pepperoni pizzas and her daughter Savannah followed with a medium size box filled with paper plates, plastic silverware, paper cups and bottles of soda.

"I am sorry that I am late, but Savannah had to pick me up so we could get here," Aunt Blanche stated as she put everything on a long folding table.

"Aunt Blanche I am going up to the first floor to see if Aunt Lynette or Aunt Sasha need anything and I will tell them that there is Pizza here.," I said.

145

"Katrina, when you see your mom do not forget to tell her and Aunt Lynette that the food is here," Floyd helped Blanche and Savanna places everything onto the table.

As she past the front desk a man was there with a younger women waiting to get their room. She was not sure if it was her Uncle Charlie since he usually travels as a bachelor. She slowly passed to get a closer look. Yes it was Uncle Charlie but who was he with this year. This year's reunion would be one to remember. Katrina made it to the elevator and pushed the button for the first floor. Katrina was actually hoping that her son Wayne was also there, but her Dad did not say anything and he was not in the conference room with the rest of their relatives.

The elevator went to the first floor and she walked toward the door that was propped slightly opened. She could hear her Aunt Sasha and Aunt Lynette laughing inside. Aunt Sasha still had eastern accent but Aunt Lynette laughed and talked with a southern drawl. She also could hear her mom in the background and a young man's voice that she did not recognize. She knocked on the room's door.

"Will you come in dear? We were just looking at the photo album your mom brought for the reunion. We were laughing at the old photos when we were so young and the Good old Days," Aunt Sasha looked up toward her.

She looked at the young man next to them it was Wayne he did come this time. She walked over and begun first hugging her oldest son, then she gave her Aunt Sasha a hug with a kiss on the cheek, she then sat next to Aunt Lynette and gave her a warm hug. Aunt Lynette was now breathing more at ease after she received her oxygen. She stood up and gave her mom a hug. She almost forgot why she was in the room.

"I am sorry I forgot the reason why I came up to your room was to let my mom know that Aunt Blanche and Savannah had brought pizza for everyone. I was also wondering Aunt Lynette if you would like some pizza or what is you ladies going to have for dinner? By the way on the way up Uncle Charlie was at the front desk checking in with a woman a little younger than him. I did not know that Uncle Charlie was seeing anyone."

"Oh Katrina that is Uncle Charlie's girl friend and he has been seeing her for almost a year. She came with him this time to meet the family," Ruthanne replied and picked up the photo album.

"I am going to bring this tomorrow during the reunion."

"Katrina do you think you can bring a slice of pizza up to us? We are tired and we are going to bed shortly. Your Aunt Lynette needs to take some of her medicine and put a breathing mask on. She wants to be ready for the reunion with renew energy," Sasha smiled at her.

"Yes I can bring some pizza up to you. Is there anything else that you need or want Aunt Lynette?"

Her Aunt Sasha held up a bottle of soda and a small bottle of Rum.

"I am not going anywhere and we are on vacation. We have everything we need. I am sure that the Pizza is probably going to cause us to have indigestion but it will be alright. Thank you sweetie and we will see you in a few minutes."

Katrina, Ruthanne, and Wayne headed to the elevator to go down to the lobby. Then they went to the conference room where other family members were gathering and talking. It was getting late and she grabbed some napkins, silverware and three slices of pizza.

"Mom, dad and Wayne I will see you tomorrow. I am taking Aunt Sasha and Aunt Lynette slices of pizza to their hotel room," she begun to walk through the lobby to the elevator. Toby was busy with guests as he waved to her. I smiled, with the pizza slices in my hand. She would need to come down to the lobby to talk to Toby when he was not so busy helping guest. She had questions to ask Toby about why Gulfport still had so much despair from the Hurricane Katrina that happened three years ago. She was looking forward to the reunion but she wanted to talk with Aunt Blanche and Uncle Willie about how their life had or not changed since that day. She was interested about why the United States government had taking their time in helping these people. Why were the people still here after losing all their belongings she just did not understand?

Katrina had been in flash floods and tornados near where she lived but nothing could prepare her from the hurricane aftermath that she would learn from the individual's that she would meet on this trip. The next day the reunion would be hosted in a small in town restaurant instead of the hotel. There she will meet more second and third cousins that was actually Aunt Blanche and Uncle Willie's grandchildren that had driven from New York. The surprise from Uncle Charlie was the announcement he made before the auction.

"Can I have everyone's attention, before I begin auctioneering? I would like you to meet my fiancé Shelby. I thought she should come with me to the reunion so she could meet the family."

Bobby Sue stood up and yelled, "hey rah go Uncle Charlie." Then everyone clapped for the new couple.

"Okay now everyone calm down. Let us get started on the auction. We have here some beautiful handmade jewelry. We will start the bidding at one cent, do I hear four cents, 50 cents, okay we have one dollar from that little lady. Do I hear $1.50? Okay sold."

Uncle Charlie continued to auctioneer the items one after another until the last one was sold. Everyone took time with their small treasures and snacked on a piece of cake. Of course the time flew bye and it was time to clean up and head back to the hotel. The family would congregate in one of the lobby areas and then around nine thirty people would head to their rooms for the night. The first group would leave after breakfast to go home or visit other friends in the area. There would be a breakfast get together and plans for the next year reunion would be decided. Relatives would slowly leave throughout the day and the last few like Ruthanne and Floyd would leave Monday afternoon for the airport to fly home. This would give her some time to talk with her Aunt Blanche. She would call her around lunch time to schedule an appointment.

It was after breakfast when she had returned back to her hotel room to take a shower and relax. The time seemed to slip away from her. It was already noon and she decided not to eat lunch instead have an early dinner. Since she would be by the shoreline maybe she would stop at a local pub to eat shrimp or crawfish. She picked up her cell phone and began to dial Aunt Blanche's number.

"Good afternoon, Aunt Blanche," she said. She could hear in the background pounding or hammering.

"I know you are busy. However, do you think this evening I could stop by to ask you a few questions pertaining to Hurricane Katrina. I was wandering if around four o'clock or four thirty would be okay?" She waited for an answer on the cell phone.

"I am sorry I can barely hear you with this racket. I have some construction workers here today until at least five o'clock. It is okay, if you don't mind the noise. I will be here this evening. We don't do much these days," she replied.

"Okay then I will see you sometime between four or four thirty," then she touched the button to end the conversation. It would give her a few hours to drive up along the shoreline to Biloxi to check out the coast and the construction of rebuilding was for others. She had some extra time to spare so she decided to go down to the pool area to sun bathe.

The pool area was quiet and no one was using the hot tub. She put on the timer for 15 minutes and she relaxed as the jets of hot water hit her back. It did feel good and she closed her eyes until she heard the timer go off. She slowly got out sitting on the chase lounge to dry off. It was just after two o'clock so she headed to her room to change into her short outfit she had laid out to wear for the afternoon. She took the elevator to the third floor. She quickly used the blow dryer on her hair and put it into a ponytail. She dressed then put some mascara on with a light floral body mist. She grabs her notebook, rental car keys, and her purse. She checked her wallet to see if she had some cash to pay for dinner, extra souvenirs and her small digital camera for those in case photo shots.

She went down the stairs to where the rental car was parked and started the adventure for the afternoon. She headed east along highway 90 along the scenic coastline road. The beaches still were ghost like only a few brave souls had came out to go swimming even though the temperature was climbing to the upper 80's. As she approached the area known as casino row in the city of Biloxi. The traffic had slowed considerably because of road construction. She now was slowed to a stop as the highway was down to one lane and waited only for a few minutes before the traffic began to pick up speed. She approached the Beau Rivage Resort and Casino it was the only one that had been rebuilt on highway 90. Then the other casino that had renovations from the 10 to 20 feet tidal surge was the Imperial Palace Resort and Casino which was on a side street just down the road. Both of them open for business and people were parking to go inside to have some evening fun. She made a right hand turn and followed the semi-circle drive by the beautiful fountain in front of the casino. She saw a few places of businesses that were open but still were having major renovations done to them. Then needed to head back on highway 90 going west. This time she noticed several large brick buildings with a large black iron gate in the front opened by the road. The buildings looked new yet there were no people or cars that she could see. It looked empty and dissolute from activity. She continued to drive at a slower speed so that she would not miss the entrance to Beauvoir Last Home Of Jefferson Davis and Museum. She approached the entrance and followed the posted signs that went onto a gravel driveway heading toward the plantation and museum. The old plantation had a large white banner over the entrance. It read "Help Beauvoir Rebuild Send Tax Deductible Donation to: Friends of Beauvoir" below in smaller print the address. The construction trailer was on the far side of the parking lot and areas were still rope or fenced off. The plantations entrance way was still gone and visitors had to use another entrance which at the time of the south was used for slaves. She walked in and put a few dollars into a slotted container then to a table where a young woman in southern style clothes from the era was taking money to view the inside.

"Good afternoon mame, the cost to view the museum is five dollars for adults, children three dollars and children under the age of two are free. Senior citizens cost is also three dollars. Please stay in the rope areas for your safety. The wall on the right has photos of what the plantation looked like before Hurricane Katrina. As you can see we still need monetary donations and have along way to go."

She took the small brochure as she was just in time for a tour. She was the last person in the group. The woman was middle aged and dressed in a southern bell dress with a bonnet.

"Good afternoon ladies and gentlemen. I am glad you are visiting the plantation. I hope you had time to look at the photo wall. I am your tour guide today and my name is Isabelle. I grew up in Biloxi and my ancestors are from the area. I will try to answer any questions at the end of the tour. As you can see the tour usually lasts about an hour but with the reconstruction it is only about twenty minutes. I apologize for that, it's because there are so many areas on the upper floors that have not been reconstructed because of wind and water damage left from Hurricane Katrina and we are in need of donations." Then Isabelle turned around to guide the group into the next set of rooms. The tour went quickly and she had only a few photos and headed outside area that once looked like a garden, instead was what was left of the confederate cemetery. She was not sure because there were some headstones broken or knocked over into tall grass section. She had taken up over an hour and she had to get going so she would not be late to see Aunt Blanche's house. She walked to the parking lot and got into the car. She then typed Aunt Blanche's address into the GPS, put her seatbelt and drove out to exit into the flow of traffic. The GPS said she had to travel about six miles west into a small town of Long Beach which was west of Gulfport and turn right. The closer she came to where she needed to turn many of the areas were concrete slabs with fencing around it. She pulled into the gravel drive way. A fifth wheeler was parked next to a electric pole. Aunt Blanche came out of the camper with a young man in his early 30's. Aunt Blanche turned toward her and waved. She got out of the car with her notebook filled with questions.

"Go ahead and go inside. I will only be a few minutes. I need to discuss something with this man about tomorrows work schedule to see if the government is going to issue an elevator and see if it's on schedule," Aunt Blanche said as she continued to walk with the worker around the outside of the bungalow style house.

"That is fine Aunt Blanche I am not in any hurry. I will meet you in the living room," She replied as she went up the staircase. The house had been placed on stilts higher than she had seen and she was sure it was from the government's new regulations for hurricane areas.

She looked out the large window that looked toward the Gulf of Mexico. The sky was a faded blue with streaks of yellow and red hues as dark clouds were blocking the sun. She heard a noise and turned around to see Aunt Blanche coming into the room with several three ring binders.

"Aunt Blanche can I help you with anything? Where is Uncle Willie I did not see him today?"

"Well Uncle Willie is in the fifth wheeler on oxygen. No, I am alright each of these binders have insurance reports, regulation criteria that all rebuilt homes have to follow, medical bills and statements for Uncle Willie, and one is for the ongoing construction companies that I have to keep hiring." Aunt Blanche stated with a sigh.

"I know the reason you wanted to talk with me was about Hurricane Katrina," she sat down in the lazy boy rocker.

"Well the first few days after Hurricane Katrina no one was allow to come home because the roads were still gone, trees and debris was everywhere the eyes could see. When we were able to return to what was left of our home. There was a smell of decay, sewage and death in the air. You're Uncle Willie and I had moved down here like other people our age to get away from the cold temperatures and snow. This was our retirement and it was all gone." As her aunt continued to tell her about the stealing of property, of mistrust of people including the aid from the government and still she had hope to rebuild a home. Aunt Blanche opened one of the three ring binders that had photos of what was left of her house and the land. They had lived in the fifth wheeler camper for the past three years. The new house was actually being slowly built and now she had some furniture in the living room.

"I belief by late August of next year, that the house will be completed and all our belongings will be in this house. As long as there are no more hurricanes like Katrina and the weather stays in our favor. We lost so much but other families lost more than their house and belongings but family members. Your Uncle Willie and I still have each other. Thank goodness my children and grandchildren were also safe. I still have hoped that those less fortunate can have their lives back," she stated as she continue to turn page after page of photos. Katrina looked each one of the photos only to see the devastation. It was still hard to comprehend what these people went through.

"I have another story to tell you about Hurricane Katrina," Aunt Blanche got up and opened a drawer in the kitchen. She came in with an old cigar box of photos. Weeks after Katrina there were people from all over the United States came to help us rebuild homes, roads, banks, churches, schools, and our city. Unfortunately, there were some that came and took advantage of us in need. I had one man say he was with a church group that would do construction. He came in did some door frames and we paid him only for what he did that day and the next day he never came back to finish the job. Then of course were those people that just took what they wanted by looting sometimes even coffins that were floating after the surge of water came into the city. The water reached up to the railroad tracks into Gulfport," Aunt Blanched sighed with sadness and her eyes were beginning to have tears.

"I am sorry; it was such an emotional time for Uncle Willie and me."

"What did the federal and state governments do to help?" I asked.

"Well the governor of the state came to see the damage and requested a state of emergency. Then the federal government sent some National Guard Units to help police the area from looters and those that were trying to rebuild. Of course later, the Federal Emergency Management Agency sent down trailers to live in for a year or so. After a year or so the F.E.M.A. came and retrieved the trailers. Since other areas in the United States were having devastating floods and weather. The trailers had to go there. Consequently, when F.E.M.A. took the trailers it would be leaving many of the people in the area homeless. Eventually, local hotels like the one you stayed in started helping families but letting them stay in them until their homes were completed," Aunt Blanched stated as she began the task of placing the photos away.

"Wow, I still cannot believe how much you went through. In fact the cities and towns in the Midwest only saw on television or heard from the news was what happened to the people in New Orleans and the Super Dome. Only the people that had communication with family or emergency facilities knew what was really going on down here. I am sorry that you had to go through this, but I am glad that you are recovering slowly to say the least," I gave my aunt a hug as we walked down the stairs of the main entrance.

"I hope that you got all of your questions answered. I need to check on Uncle Willie and start making something to eat. My oldest daughter is stopping by tonight with some groceries," Aunt Blanched gave her another hug and went into the fifth wheeler camper.

She decided that she would take a walk down to the beach and for evening stroll before trying to find a local restaurant. The sun was beginning to set off to the horizon and the waves of the Gulf of Mexico caressed the sand. She did not see any pelicans, sea gulls, or animal life. There were just some remnants of a jelly fish on the shore. The area still looked empty. She walked back to the car and left to go to an area where some fishing docks had been built. There were only a few shrimp boats in the Pass Christian Harbor. She parked the car in a gravel parking lot to see if the restaurant at the end of the dock was opened for business. She went to the door only to see the sign saying in big letters "STILL REBUILDING DO TO HURRICANE KATRINA". She returned to the car and went back out to the main road highway 90 heading toward the small towns named the Bay of St. Louis and Waveland. Initially, this was where the actual eye of Hurricane Katrina made landfall and most of the storm surge went up into the bay. She turned down a road that looked like it might go to the old Bay of Saint Louis downtown area. The restaurant was small and had an old metal Coca-Cola from another time on the side of the building. She was lucky to find the place open for business. There were several people sitting at the booths enjoying dinner. The waitress came over to her and gave her a menu.

"You can sit anywhere and fresh shrimp came today. So we are serving our favorite shrimp basket or fish and chips. I am your waitress and my name is Charlotte but call me Char. There are days we don't have shrimp because the area is still recovering from Hurricane Katrina and then a year later the other hurricane."

"Thank you! Yes, I would like your famous shrimp basket along with a beer and a glass of water," she replied. She began reading a local paper that had been in a stand near the restaurant entrance. Her dinner arrived and she put the newspaper down. Before long she was finished with her meal and walked out the door. She looked down the street only to see a poster that said "WE NEED WATER AND FOOD" that was by a foundation of a house that was never rebuilt. She decided to head back to the hotel that evening. She walked to her car and noticed that a church's steeple was still on the ground, but people were using the church for services anyway. She could hear them singing gospel songs as she got into her rental car. She went back to highway 90 to head east toward Long Beach and Gulfport. As I drove east, along the road the large trees looked like skeletons. Many of the trees still had parts of houses embedded or entwined in them, as new leaves were trying to grow. Houses that still had the letter X mark in red or a number which indicated the dead. The darkness of night was approaching and I turn on my headlights. The old beat up tugboat that had been placed on shore from Hurricane Camille 1969 and the souvenir shop that was built next to it had been washed away by Hurricane Katrina. Yet the old tug boat stays put as people enter the city of Gulfport. People will come back to rebuild as they have in the past. Life will return to the neighborhoods, the towns and cities like they did before by never giving up and living on as this is part of the human nature in all of us. We never give up only to have hope along with the faith that we can build and rebuild a stronger future. We will do whatever it takes so the next time we can be stronger emotional and physically for what comes our way. We will deal with the next disaster whether it is emotionally, physically or both by having the hope that we can rebuild that friendship or that building one at a time to make our life better and normal. As human beings we continue to have hope and that we will learn from the mistakes we have made only to prepare us individually or as a country to survive for a better tomorrow.

Hope

"Of all the forces that make for a better world,
none is so powerful as hope,
With hope, one can think, one can work, one can dream.
If you have hope, you have everything."

Written by unknown author

"**Y**ES OF COURSE, they are here to rebuild the roads and the Gulf shoreline from the hurricane three years ago. Here mame is your room card key. I am here today until nine o'clock tonight and I will be back here tomorrow morning around ten."

"Thank you and I am sure that I will be fine," she took her card key and went to the elevator. She would go to her room and freshen up before seeing what everyone else was doing the rest of the night.

She put on a summer dress then went out of the room to the elevator. The elevator door opened and she went in push the close button also the lobby button. The elevator door opened into the lobby and she turned left toward the conference room. The door was propped open and she saw her dad Floyd sitting at one of the tables with one of his sisters. This was the only time she was able to see her relatives. She noticed that several of the had made it in for the occasion.

"Hi; when did you and Mom get in today?"

"We got in around noon. Your mom went up to the first floor to see your Aunt Lynette. She is in room 132 with your Aunt Sasha. They are sharing the room to save on expenses. Also your Aunt Lynette might need some help," he replied.

"Well I will go up to see Aunt Lynette and Aunt Sasha to see if they need anything. What are you doing for dinner tonight?"

Just as Katrina was to leave her Aunt Blanche walked into the room with three large pepperoni pizzas and her daughter Savannah followed with a medium size box filled with paper plates, plastic silverware, paper cups and bottles of soda.

"I am sorry that I am late, but Savannah had to pick me up so we could get here," Aunt Blanche stated as she put everything on a long folding table.

"Aunt Blanche I am going up to the first floor to see if Aunt Lynette or Aunt Sasha need anything and I will tell them that there is Pizza here.," I said.

"Katrina, when you see your mom do not forget to tell her and Aunt Lynette that the food is here," Floyd helped Blanche and Savanna places everything onto the table.

As she past the front desk a man was there with a younger women waiting to get their room. She was not sure if it was her Uncle Charlie since he usually travels as a bachelor. She slowly passed to get a closer look. Yes it was Uncle Charlie but who was he with this year. This year's reunion would be one to remember. Katrina made it to the elevator and pushed the button for the first floor. Katrina was actually hoping that her son Wayne was also there, but her Dad did not say anything and he was not in the conference room with the rest of their relatives.

The elevator went to the first floor and she walked toward the door that was propped slightly opened. She could hear her Aunt Sasha and Aunt Lynette laughing inside. Aunt Sasha still had eastern accent but Aunt Lynette laughed and talked with a southern drawl. She also could hear her mom in the background and a young man's voice that she did not recognize. She knocked on the room's door.

"Will you come in dear? We were just looking at the photo album your mom brought for the reunion. We were laughing at the old photos when we were so young and the Good old Days," Aunt Sasha looked up toward her.

She looked at the young man next to them it was Wayne he did come this time. She walked over and begun first hugging her oldest son, then she gave her Aunt Sasha a hug with a kiss on the cheek, she then sat next to Aunt Lynette and gave her a warm hug. Aunt Lynette was now breathing more at ease after she received her oxygen. She stood up and gave her mom a hug. She almost forgot why she was in the room.

"I am sorry I forgot the reason why I came up to your room was to let my mom know that Aunt Blanche and Savannah had brought pizza for everyone. I was also wondering Aunt Lynette if you would like some pizza or what is you ladies going to have for dinner? By the way on the way up Uncle Charlie was at the front desk checking in with a woman a little younger than him. I did not know that Uncle Charlie was seeing anyone."

"Oh Katrina that is Uncle Charlie's girl friend and he has been seeing her for almost a year. She came with him this time to meet the family," Ruthanne replied and picked up the photo album.

"I am going to bring this tomorrow during the reunion."

"Katrina do you think you can bring a slice of pizza up to us? We are tired and we are going to bed shortly. Your Aunt Lynette needs to take some of her medicine and put a breathing mask on. She wants to be ready for the reunion with renew energy," Sasha smiled at her.

"Yes I can bring some pizza up to you. Is there anything else that you need or want Aunt Lynette?"

Her Aunt Sasha held up a bottle of soda and a small bottle of Rum.

"I am not going anywhere and we are on vacation. We have everything we need. I am sure that the Pizza is probably going to cause us to have indigestion but it will be alright. Thank you sweetie and we will see you in a few minutes."

Katrina, Ruthanne, and Wayne headed to the elevator to go down to the lobby. Then they went to the conference room where other family members were gathering and talking. It was getting late and she grabbed some napkins, silverware and three slices of pizza.

"Mom, dad and Wayne I will see you tomorrow. I am taking Aunt Sasha and Aunt Lynette slices of pizza to their hotel room," she begun to walk through the lobby to the elevator. Toby was busy with guests as he waved to her. I smiled, with the pizza slices in my hand. She would need to come down to the lobby to talk to Toby when he was not so busy helping guest. She had questions to ask Toby about why Gulfport still had so much despair from the Hurricane Katrina that happened three years ago. She was looking forward to the reunion but she wanted to talk with Aunt Blanche and Uncle Willie about how their life had or not changed since that day. She was interested about why the United States government had taking their time in helping these people. Why were the people still here after losing all their belongings she just did not understand?

Katrina had been in flash floods and tornados near where she lived but nothing could prepare her from the hurricane aftermath that she would learn from the individual's that she would meet on this trip. The next day the reunion would be hosted in a small in town restaurant instead of the hotel. There she meets more second and third cousins that was actually Aunt Blanche and Uncle Willie's grandchildren that had driven from upstate New York. The surprise from Uncle Charlie was the announcement he made before the auction.

"Can I have everyone's attention, before I begin auctioneering? I would like you to meet my fiancé Shelby. I thought she should come with me to the reunion so she could meet the family."

Bobby Sue stood up and yelled, "hey rah go Uncle Charlie." Then everyone clapped for the new couple.

"Okay now everyone calm down. Let us get started on the auction. We have here some beautiful handmade jewelry. We will start the bidding at one cent, do I hear four cents, 50 cents, okay we have one dollar from that little lady. Do I hear $1.50? Okay sold."

Uncle Charlie continued to auctioneer the items one after another until the last one was sold. Everyone took time with their small treasures and snacked on a piece of cake. Of course the time flew bye and it was time to clean up and head back to the hotel. The family would congregate in one of the lobby areas and then around nine thirty people would head to their rooms for the night. The first group would leave after breakfast to go home or visit other friends in the area. There would be a breakfast get together and plans for the next year reunion would be decided. Relatives would slowly leave throughout the day and the last few like Ruthanne and Floyd would leave Monday afternoon for the airport to fly home. This would give her some time to talk with her Aunt Blanche. She would call her around lunch time to schedule an appointment.

It was after breakfast when she had returned back to her hotel room to take a shower and relax. The time seemed to slip away from her. It was already noon and she decided not to each lunch instead have an early dinner. Since she would be by the shoreline maybe stop at a local pub to eat shrimp or crawfish. She picked up her cell phone and began to dial Aunt Blanche's number.

"Good afternoon, Aunt Blanche," she said. She could hear in the background pounding or hammering.

"I know you are busy. However, do you think this evening I could stop by to ask you a few questions pertaining to Hurricane Katrina. I was wandering if around four o'clock or four thirty would be okay?" She waited for an answer on the cell phone.

"I am sorry I can barely hear you with this entire racket. I have some construction workers here today until at least five o'clock. It is okay, if you don't mind the noise. I will be here this evening. We don't do much these days." She relied.

"Okay then I will see sometime between four and four thirty," then she touched the button to end the conversation. It would give her a few hours to drive up along the shoreline to Biloxi to check out the coast and the construction of rebuilding was going for others. She had some time to spare so she decided to go down to the pool area to sun bathe.

The pool area was quiet and no one was using the hot tub. She put on the time for 15 minutes and she relaxed as the jets of hot water hit her back. It did feel good and she closed her eyes until she heard the timer go off. She slowly got out sitting on the chase lounge to dry off. It was just after two o'clock so she headed to her room to change into the short outfit she had out to wear for the afternoon. She took the elevator to the third floor. She quickly used the blow dryer on her hair and put it into a ponytail. She dressed then put some mascara on with a light floral body mist. She grabs her notebook, rental car keys, and her purse. She checked her wallet to see if she had some cash to pay for dinner along extra souvenirs and her small digital camera for those just in case photo shots.

She went down the stairs to where the rental car was parked and started the adventure for the afternoon. She headed east along highway 90 along the scenic coastline road. The beaches still were ghost like only a few brave souls had came out to go swimming even though the temperature was climbing to the upper 80's. As she approached the area known as casino row in the city of Biloxi. The traffic had slowed considerably because of road construction. She now was slowed to a stop as the highway was down to one lane and waited only for a few minutes before the traffic began to pick up speed. She was at the Beau Rivage Resort and Casino it was the only one on highway 90 that had been rebuilt. The other casino that had renovations from the 10 to 20 feet tidal surge was the Imperial Palace Resort and Casino but it was on a side street just down the road. They were open for business and people were parking to go inside to eat a buffet and do some gambling at the card tables or slots. She made a right hand turn and followed the semi-circle drive by the beautiful fountain in front of the casino to turn around. She saw a few places that were open but still were having major renovations done to them. She needed to head back on highway 90 going west. This time she noticed several large brick buildings with a large black iron gate in the front opened by the road. The buildings looked new yet there were no people or cars that see could see if it was open. It looked empty and dissolute from activity. She continued to drive at a slower speed so that she would not miss the entrance to Beauvoir Last Home Of Jefferson Davis and Museum. She approached the entrance and followed the posted signs that went onto a gravel driveway heading toward the plantation and museum. The old plantation had a large white banner over the entrance. It read "Help Beauvoir Rebuild Send Tax Deductible Donation to: Friends of Beauvoir" below in smaller print the address. The construction trailer was on the far side of the parking lot and areas were still rope or fenced off. The plantations entrance way was still gone and visitors had to use another entrance which at the time of the south was used for slaves. She walked in and put a few dollars into a slotted container then to a table where a young woman in southern style clothes from the era was taking money to view the inside.

"Good afternoon mame, the cost to view the museum is five dollars for adults, children three dollars and children under the age of two are free. Senior citizens cost is also three dollars. Please stay in the rope areas it is for your safety. The wall on the right has photos of what the plantation looked like before Hurricane Katrina and after Katrina. As you can see we still need monetary donations and long way to go."

She took the small brochure as she was just in time for a tour. She was the last person in the group. The woman was middle aged and dressed in a southern bell dress with a bonnet.

"Good afternoon ladies and gentlemen. I am glad you are visiting the plantation. I hope you had time to look at the photo wall. I am your tour guide today and my name is Isabelle. I grew up in Biloxi and my ancestors are from the area. I will try to answer any questions at the end of the tour. As you can see the tour usually lasts about an hour but with the reconstruction it is only about twenty minutes. I apologize for that it is because there are so many areas of the upper floors that have not been reconstructed because of wind and water damage left from Hurricane

Katrina and we are in need of donations." Then Isabelle turned around to guide the group into the next set of rooms. The tour went quickly and she had only taken a few photos and headed outside to an area that once looked like a garden but it was what was left of the confederate cemetery. She was not sure because there were some headstones broken or knocked over into a tall grass section. She had taken up over an hour and she had to get going so she would not be late to see Aunt Blanche's house. She walked to the parking lot and got into the car. She then typed Aunt Blanche's address into the GPS, put her seatbelt and drove out to exit into the flow of traffic. The GPS said she had to travel about six miles west into a small town of Long Beach which was west of Gulfport and turn right. The closer she came to where she needed to turn many of the areas were concrete slabs with fencing around it. She pulled into the gravel drive way. A fifth wheeler was parked next to pole with electric. Aunt Blanche came out of the camper with a young man in his early 30's. Aunt Blanche turned toward her and waved. She got of the car with her notebook filled with questions.

"Go ahead and go inside. I will only be a few minutes. I need to discuss something with this man about tomorrows work schedule and to see if the government issued elevator is still coming on schedule," Aunt Blanche said as she continued to walk with the worker around the outside of the bungalow style house.

"That is fine Aunt Blanche I am not in any hurry. I will meet you in the living room," She replied as she went up the staircase. The house had been placed on stilts higher than she had seen and she was sure it was from the government's new regulations for hurricane areas.

She looked out the large window that looked toward the Gulf of Mexico. The sky was a faded blue with streaks of yellow and red hues as dark clouds were blocking the sun. She heard a noise and turned around to see Aunt Blanche coming into the room with several three ring binders.

"Aunt Blanche can I help you with anything? Where is Uncle Willie I did not see him today?"

"Well Uncle Willie is in the fifth wheeler on oxygen. No I am alright each of these binders have insurance reports, regulation criteria that all rebuilt homes have to follow, medical bills and statements for Uncle Willie, and one is for the ongoing construction companies that I have to keep hiring." Aunt Blanche stated with a sigh.

"I know the reason you wanted to talk with me was about Hurricane Katrina," she sat down in the lazy boy rocker.

"Well the first few days after Hurricane Katrina no one was allow to come home because the roads were still gone, trees and debris was everywhere the eyes could see. When we were able to return to what was left of our home. There was a smell of decay, sewage and death in the air. You're Uncle Willie and I had moved down here like other people our age to get away from the cold temperatures and snow. This was our retirement and it was all gone." As her aunt continued to tell her about the stealing of property, of mistrust of people including the aid from the government and still she had hope to rebuild a home. Aunt Blanche opened one of the three ring binders that had photos of what was left of her house and the land. They had lived in the fifth wheeler camper for the past three years. The new house was actually being slowly built and now she had some furniture in the living room.

"I belief by late August of next year, that the house will be completed and all our belongings will be in this house. As long as there are no more hurricanes like Katrina and the weather stays in our favor. We lost so much but other families lost more than their house and belongings but family members. Your Uncle Willie and I still have each other. Thank goodness my children and grandchildren were also safe. I still have hoped that those less fortunate can have their lives back," she stated as she continue to turn page after page of photos. Katrina looked each one of the photos only to see the devastation. It was still hard to comprehend what these people went through.

"I have another story to tell you about Hurricane Katrina," Aunt Blanche got up and opened a drawer in the kitchen. She came in with an old cigar box of photos. Weeks after Katrina there were people from all over the United States came to help us rebuild homes, roads, banks, churches, schools, and our city. Unfortunately, there were some that came and took advantage of us in need. I had one man say he was with a church group that would do construction. He came in did some door frames and we paid him only for what he did that day and the next day he never came back to finish the job. Then of course were those people that just took what they wanted by looting sometimes even coffins that were floating after the surge of water came into the city. The water reached up to the railroad tracks into Gulfport," Aunt Blanched sighed with sadness and her eyes were beginning to have tears.

"I am sorry; it was such an emotional time for Uncle Willie and me."

"What did the federal and state governments do to help?" I asked.

"Well the governor of the state came to see the damage and requested a state of emergency. Then the federal government sent some National Guard Units to help police the area from looters and those that were trying to rebuild. Of course later, the Federal Emergency Management Agency sent down trailers to live in for a year or so. After a year or so the F.E.M.A. came and retrieved the trailers. Since other areas in the United States were having devastating floods and weather. The trailers had to go there. Consequently, when F.E.M.A. took the trailers it would be leaving many of the people in the area homeless. Eventually, local hotels like the one you stayed in started helping families but letting them stay in them until their homes were completed," Aunt Blanched stated as she began the task of placing the photos away.

"Wow, I still cannot believe how much you went through. In fact the cities and towns in the Midwest only saw on television or heard from the news was what happened to the people in New Orleans and the Super Dome. Only the people that had communication with family or emergency facilities knew what was really going on down here. I am sorry that you had to go through this, but I am glad that you are recovering slowly to say the least," I gave my aunt a hug as we walked down the stairs of the main entrance.

"I hope that you got all of your questions answered. I need to check on Uncle Willie and start making something to eat. My oldest daughter is stopping by tonight with some groceries," Aunt Blanched gave her another hug and went into the fifth wheeler camper.

She decided that she would take a walk down to the beach and for evening stroll before trying to find a local restaurant. The sun was beginning to set off to the horizon and the waves of the Gulf of Mexico caressed the sand. She did not see any pelicans, sea gulls, or animal life. There were just some remnants of a jelly fish on the shore. The area still looked empty. She walked back to the car and left to go to an area where some fishing docks had been built. There were only a few shrimp boats in the Pass Christian Harbor. She parked the car in a gravel parking lot to see if the restaurant at the end of the dock was opened for business. She went to the door only to see the sign saying in big letters "STILL REBUILDING DO TO HURRICANE KATRINA". She returned to the car and went back out to the main road highway 90 heading toward the small towns named the Bay of St. Louis and Waveland. Initially, this was where the actual eye of Hurricane Katrina made landfall and most of the storm surge went up into the bay. She turned down a road that looked like it might go to the old Bay of Saint Louis downtown area. The restaurant was small and had an old metal Coca-Cola from another time on the side of the building. She was lucky to find the place open for business. There were several people sitting at the booths enjoying dinner. The waitress came over to her and gave her a menu.

"You can sit anywhere and fresh shrimp came today. So we are serving our favorite shrimp basket or fish and chips. I am your waitress and my name is Charlotte but call me Char. There are days we don't have shrimp because the area is still recovering from Hurricane Katrina and then a year later the other hurricane."

"Thank you! Yes I would like your famous shrimp basket along with a beer and a glass of water," she replied. She began reading a local paper that had been in a stand near the restaurant entrance. Her dinner arrived and she put the newspaper down. Before long she was finished with her meal and walked out the door. She looked down the street only to see a poster like sign that said "WE NEED WATER AND FOOD" that was by a foundation of a house that was never rebuilt. She needed to head back to the hotel that evening. She walked to the car and noticed that a church's steeple was still on the ground, but people were using the church for services anyway. She could hear them singing gospel songs as she got into her rental car. She went back to highway 90 to head east toward Long Beach and Gulfport. As I drove east on there were large trees along the road that looked like skeletons some still had parts of houses embedded or entwined as new leaves were trying to grow. Houses that still had the letter X in red or a number which indicated the dead. The darkness of night was approaching and I turn on my headlights. The old beat up tugboat that had been placed on shore from Hurricane Camille 1969 and the souvenir shop that was built next to it had been washed away by Hurricane Katrina. Yet the old tug boat stays put as people enter the city of Gulfport. People will come back to rebuild as they have in the past. Life will return to the neighborhoods, the towns and cities like they did before by never giving up and living on as this is part of the human nature in all of us. We never give up only to have hope along with faith that we can build and rebuild a stronger future. We will do whatever it takes so that the next time we can be stronger emotional and physically for what comes our way. We will deal with the next disaster whether it is emotionally, physically or both by having the hope that we can rebuild that friendship or that building one at a time to make our life better and normal. As human beings we continue to have hoped and that we will learn from the mistakes we have made only to prepare us individually or as a country to survive for a better tomorrow.

Hope

"Of all the forces that make for a better world,
none is so powerful as hope,
With hope, one can think, one can work, one can dream.
If you have hope, you have everything."

Written by unknown author

Printed in the United States
By Bookmasters